Dani Elias

Blossom with Me

Fellside Mountain Rescue Series
Book 1

Editor: Sofia Artola Diaz

This is a work of fiction. Names, characters, organisations, places, events and incidents are either products of the author's imagination or are used fictitiously. Any resemblance to actual persons, living or dead, or actual events is purely coincidental.

Contact Dani Elias at d.elias@daniebooks.com for permission

Blossom with Me

Chapter 1

Alex

"Right, guys, I need a volunteer," Tommy announces. He is the leader of the Fellside Mountain Rescue Volunteers team I am part of. Tommy looks around the tiny break room, which doubles as a meeting room for us to come together for our weekly meetings and general debriefs after a rescue mission.

"There are three new shops in town, and I need someone to go and convince the owners to let us put a donation collection box up," he explains. He rattles one of the plastic boxes shaped like a mountain in front of him to emphasise his request. Silence is the only thing he gets in response.

I look at the guys around the table. We all volunteer for Fellside Mountain Rescue, or FMR, as we usually shorten it, acting as mountain rescuers in addition to our day job. And we all love it and are proud to give our time to help others.

"Anyone?" Tommy asks again and looks at us expectantly. "Come on, I am not asking for the world. And you all know we need the funding." He tries to put pressure on us. We don't charge the people we rescue for our service. Consequently, FMR is always underfunded, and we rely on donations to keep us going. This means we all have to help get the funding to keep FMR alive. And we really don't enjoy that part of our role. We host regular fundraising events and have the support from a few corporate donors to help us pay for our equipment. Tommy also had the genius idea to put collection boxes in shops around the village. Most local shopkeepers are professionals in guilting tourists to spare a penny or two for FMR. This way, we get at least some of our money back from those who we later have to rescue.

"Susan Miller's daughter just opened a bakery. Extreme Sports opened a new shop next to the church. And some lady from London has taken over Estelle's flower shop on Fell

1

Road. If nobody volunteers, I will pick someone." Tommy threatens in a last-ditch attempt to convince someone to carry out the hated task.

We are not salespeople, and we all loathe trying to convince someone, especially those who come to our village from the big cities and try to turn it into a hipster place, of how important our work is. I have been told a few times by a London escapee, aka someone who had enough of the big city life and is trying to make a new start here, that the cheap FMR collection tins don't fit their shop style.

"I believe it is Phil's turn," Nick pipes up. I feel Phil shift uncomfortably next to me, and I give Nick a stern look. Nick and I have learned to get along when it comes to rescues, but he can be an absolute arsehole away from the mountains. We haven't seen eye to eye since our school days. He always seems to want to outdo me. Life is a constant competition to him. How someone like this was allowed to become a teacher is beyond me. I worry about the ideas he puts in the children's heads, although my Granny, who sits on the school board, assured me that he is an extremely popular teacher.

When he can't find an opportunity to pick on me, he will go after Phil. Phil has been my best friend since we ran into each other on top of a mountain and had to set up a makeshift bivouac during a terrible storm that hit out of nowhere. I had seen Phil around the village growing up, but he was a few years younger than me, so we had not been hanging out together as kids. He works as a handy man and jack of all trades at one of the National Trust places not far from Fellside. A job that suits him, given how notoriously shy he can be. Any customer-facing job would have been a nightmare for him. We all accept that he wants to stay out of the limelight, and when it comes to our annual fundraising events, we let him deal with the technical work in the background. He can only conquer his shyness when we are out in the mountains trying to find yet another lost soul. The drive to help someone at risk helps him overcome all barriers. He is one of our best at showing empathy with injured hikers and has a talent to keep them calm. But talking to strangers about donations is definitely not his forte.

"Alex, didn't you say you are off today? You couldn't just take one hour to quickly jump into these shops?" Phil asks casually, but I can hear the pleading in his voice. Before I can answer, Tommy interrupts.

"You will have to learn at some point, Phil. You can't always hide in the shadow. Alex, why don't you tag along, and if he panics, you can take over." I give Tommy a sharp look to show him I am not impressed. Why do we suddenly force Phil into a role we all know will cause him massive anxiety? Nick probably complained to Tommy behind our backs that Phil wasn't contributing enough. I don't need to see the smug look on Nick's face to know that I am right. He really is a twat.

"Works for me," I reply, trying not to show how annoyed I am. This would just play into Nick's hands, and I am not giving him that satisfaction.

I can feel Phil relax next to me. He knows I will never force him to do anything he is uncomfortable with, so my tagging along takes the pressure off him.

"Excellent. Have a good day everyone!" Tommy ends the meeting and puts the three collection boxes and a list with the three addresses in front of me on the table. The rest of the guys can't clear out quick enough.

"Well, thanks very much, you twat." Phil hisses at Nick as we catch up with him in the corridor. The little weasel just shrugs with a big grin.

"Have fun," he says sarcastically before quickly exiting the building. I just shake my head. There is no point in starting an argument with Nick. It is just what he wants.

"Thanks, mate!" Phil says as we walk out of the rescue centre, which is housed on the outskirts of the village.

"Well, not what I had planned for my hard-earned day off," I sigh. I own a carpentry business and work long hours five days a week. Occasionally, when I finish a large project or have a gap between big jobs, I allow myself an extra day off. I employ Richard, a seasoned carpenter who works part-time, and Gary, a young apprentice. When I am not there, Richard can oversee the work on smaller projects we are currently working on, answer the phone and ensure Gary doesn't burn down the workshop. Gary is a clever boy but sometimes a bit too enthusiastic. He reminds me a lot of myself when I was eighteen.

"Oh, come on, what else would you have to do?" Phil asks. "Your latest bed warmer is probably not available during the day, and your climbing buddy," pointing at himself, "is busy handing out collection boxes. So, you have nothing to do, really."

"I do other things aside from shagging and climbing. And for the record, I haven't had anyone in my bed in weeks." I retort, slightly annoyed that my best friend doesn't think more of me. But then, can I really blame him? I am known to be a tag'em and drop'em kind of guy.

"I did notice that," Phil says. "And why is that? All shagged out?" he chuckles. I shrug and ruffle my short curly hair. The truth is that I am ready to settle down with a special someone, build a home and live happily ever after. I am not quite sure if I am prepared to admit that though.

"I'm just bored with the women in this village, and frankly, I want more than just a one-night stand with a tourist," I admit hesitantly, testing the waters. If you can't open up to your best friend, who can you open to, right?

"That's a whole new side to you. Looking for the happily ever after?" Phil snickers. I just shrug once again and walk over to my Range Rover.

"Get in," is my only reply as I unlock the car with the button on the key. Phil climbs into the passenger seat. I can see on his face that he would like to dig deeper, but he lets it go. Like many men, talking about feelings is not really our thing. Sometimes I do envy women.

The first shop on our list is Cherry Pie Bakery. The owner, Lisa, is a couple of years older than Phil and me. Nevertheless, as she grew up in Fellside, we have often crossed paths. I vaguely remember having a one-night stand with her about ten years ago. Now she is married to a banker who commutes to Manchester for work. We don't really hang around in the same circle, but we might occasionally see her in the pub with her husband.

Luckily for Phil and me, her brother was a rescuer until he moved to Newcastle. He still hangs out with us when he comes back to visit his family. Lisa knows how vital FMR is, and is only too happy to take some money from tourists to help us keep the operation running.

"Well done us," Phil declares through a mouthful of éclair. Lisa insisted we take some of the cream-filled pastries, and who are we to turn down free food?

I chuckle and correct him, "Well done me, you mean, given that you didn't utter a word." He has the decency to blush before shrugging and stuffing his mouth with the rest of the éclair.

We walk the short distance to Extreme Sports. The small company has shops selling climbing gear in most of the tourist centres in the Lake District and has just opened its second outlet in Fellside. Not sure why they need two, as Fellside is a small village. You can walk from one end to the other in less than 45 minutes. The irony is not lost on me that we need a second shop, so people don't have to walk too far when buying their walking gear.

Phil takes the lead on this pitch to sell our mission, mainly because the guy on the till had previously worked with him. We are in and out of there in five minutes.

That leaves one shop, the florist. To be honest, it is not really a new shop: it has been here for years. However, it is under new ownership. I have heard that Estelle, the previous proprietor, finally retired and is exploring the countries along the Silk Road. She is in her late seventies and has long been talking about travelling, but her shop kept her hostage. Her daughter had moved to London in her twenties, married a rich guy and refused to come back up north. If Estelle wanted to see her family, she had to travel down to London, which she did as often as the shop would allow her to. My own grandmother was good friends with Estelle and had ranted about this more than once at our monthly Harris family dinners. The thought alone that Estelle's daughter had moved so far away horrified my Granny. There is no way she would have allowed this to happen in our family, not that any of us ever had the desire to leave the Lake District. My whole family still lives no more than 45 minutes drive from Fellside and is not planning to change that. Neither of us went to university and there was no other reason to move away from this place we love so much. We are a working-class family through and through, and the Lake District is our home.

Estelle's old shop is not far from the church in the centre of the village. I have walked pass it a million times. When she did some refurbishment work a few years ago, my Granny convinced Estelle to use me for the carpentry work. And, in return, she talked me into giving Estelle a very, very generous discount. Estelle repaid me in kind by filling me up with biscuits and cake every day I was there. She was always a great supporter of FMR, but she closed her shop a year ago and must have returned the collection box as part of the closure.

Now that I think about it, Granny mentioned at our last lunch that Estelle's granddaughter had taken over the shop. But I can't be sure as I was watching rugby on TV then, and rugby takes priority over everything for Harris men.

Frankly, that's what I would like to be doing right now, watch some rugby. Let's just hope this woman will not cause a fuss, and we can get out of there quickly. The Six Nations cup is on, and I know Phil will also be itching to head to the pub for a pint and watch the best sport in the world.

Chapter 2

Emma

It is dark and cool in the backroom of the small shop. Correction, my shop. Well, mine and Christina's shop. When Nana announced her retirement and that she was looking to sell her shop, I couldn't stop thinking about it: moving away from London, a city I loathe; having a better work-life balance; working with flowers rather than twisting the law to make even more profits for some corrupt corporation… that just sounded too tempting. At that time, I was a corporate lawyer in one of the biggest law firms in London. My mother was proud of me, whilst I hated it. My mother left the Lake District when she was young and became a fully fledged city girl. She loves everything about London. After all, she can afford a lavish life with the money my father brings home. Everything looks golden if you live in an ivory tower.

Despite never leaving London when I was young, or maybe because of it, I always longed for a life in the countryside. My grandmother knew how much I hated my job, so she convinced me to come and take a break up here last summer. I fell in love with Fellside the minute I arrived, so it was not difficult for her to persuade me to take over the shop. When I refused to take it for free (after all, she needed the funds for her travels), she made me a very generous offer that I couldn't turn down.

I had done floristry as a hobby for a few years, probably because I subconsciously wanted the life my Nana told me so much about. In one of the courses, I met Christina, my crazy best friend who is now co-owning the shop with me. She took the floristry course hoping to open her own business one day. So, when my grandmother offered to sign over her shop to me, not only did Christina push me to take the offer, but she proposed to become my partner. Not having to do this on my own made me feel a lot more comfortable, especially as I am a lot better working in the background with all my social anxiety, whilst Christina can charm any room with her natural liveliness.

Both of our families threw a fit when we announced our intention. My mother did not understand why I would give up a well-paid job for a shop that would pay me less than half of what I was earning as a lawyer. And to add insult to injury, the shop was located in a village she hated. But then, I wasn't surprised by her reaction. My mother and I don't have a good relationship. In her eyes, I am a complete failure. Being a lawyer was the only thing she liked about me.

Christina's mother hadn't left London since she had come to England from Eastern Europe just before Christina was born. Just like my mother, she couldn't understand why anyone would want to move away from it. Although Christina's family is firmly cemented in the working class and doesn't enjoy the same luxurious life as my mother, growing up in Poland, Christina's mum had always dreamed of the shining city of London. Making it in London was her greatest achievement.

Despite our families' objections, we did it anyway and couldn't wait to leave the noise of London behind. So, three months ago, we packed up and came up here. We now both own a little cottage for a fraction of the cost of what a broom cupboard in London would set us back. Despite my lawyer's salary, I had been house-sharing in London, so having my own space now is a dream come true. I am introverted and get my energy from being on my own: naturally, I cherish the new life that allows me to just sit in my little living room, put my feet up and get lost in a good book. No legal deadline looming, and no noisy housemates returning drunk from yet another pub crawl. I can even walk around naked without the fear of traumatising an unexpectant housemate. Don't judge me!

Christina also loves the newfound freedom, having shared a house with her mum and two brothers until we moved up north. And she loves the commute. No more being stuck for two hours in a packed underground train whilst paying a fortune for this less-than-adequate service. Her place is only ten-minutes from the shop. My cottage is around the corner, a mere two-minute walk away. I definitely won the commuter jackpot.

When it comes to the shop, we have divided the duties. I am a brilliant organiser—give me a spreadsheet and I will be happy. I also have a talent for finances, so the shop's bookkeeping isn't causing me a lot of difficulties.

Christina manages the shop front. Talking husbands into beautiful bouquets rather than the three pathetic roses they had planned to buy has become second nature to her.

She has dark hair, but she always adds another colour to it. Currently, streaks of lilac mix with her dark brown curls. She appears graceful whatever she does and has a bubbly personality that fills every room with joy. Her slim figure, with curves at just the right spots, makes her a natural beauty that draws people in.

On the other hand, I am all curves, and not in a good way, as my mother keeps reminding me. I usually hid my plump figure under dark, baggy clothes. My hair is a gold blond with a natural wave to it—probably my only redeeming feature. I am taller than Christina, and my height makes me appear even bigger than my curves alone do. Unlike Christina, I hate being the centre of attention. So for me, hiding away in the back, working on the flowers and spreadsheets, is the natural role to fill. Of course, whenever Christina is out to deliver flowers or when she has a day off, I also have to manage the shop floor, and that is definitely my least favourite part of our business.

"Listen, we have been in this town for over three months and never been to the pub. I really want to go. I haven't flirted with anyone except old Mr Burgess," Christina complains from the shop floor, where she is rearranging the buckets with flowers to hide the empty spot left behind by the bouquet she just sold.

I snort. Mr Burgess is in his 60s and comes once a week to buy his wife some flowers. Christina rendered him speechless the first time she showed her flirtatious side. He left the shop with a bright red face and a bouquet double the price he had planned to pay.

"You have never shied away from going out on the pull alone," I shout back at her from the back of the shop, where I am adding some finishing touches to the bouquet in my hand.

In fact, I don't go out on the pull, full stop. I am not the person that gets hit on. Usually, I am just the friend who gets ditched when the person with me finds a hook-up. To be honest, that's more what my other friends kept doing to me. Not Christina though: she may flirt a little, but whenever someone hits on her when we are out, she gives him her number and then shoos him away with the promise that she will answer should he call.

"Firstly, who said anything about hooking up? I talked about flirting. If more comes of it, that is just an added bonus. And secondly, when have you been on a date the last time? Let me think," Christina appears in the doorway between the shop and the backroom. She dramatically scrunches her face as if searching her brain for an answer to her own question.

"Emma, I have known you for three years, and in all that time, you have never been on a date. So it is time." She announces, feigning shock. We have had this conversation many times. She thinks that if I wanted to, I could have lots of guys asking me out. Well, experience has taught me otherwise. My so-called friends in London have always told me that I am "too picky" and that I should settle for what I can get. And by that, they meant that I have no chance with nice, good looking or interesting men, and should instead look for some boring sleaze balls because those kind of men just take about anyone. Looking at the very short list of ex-boyfriends I have had, they were not so wrong. And I appreciate the honesty, but the optimist in me just doesn't want to give up on maybe finding my dream guy after all.

I carry the red and purple bouquet I just finished to the front of the shop and put it in a bucket near the door.

"Firstly, you know how I turn into a complete idiot around guys, especially guys I find attractive," I reply and walk up to the counter where customers typically stand when paying for their flowers. Christina snorts loudly.

"Yes, I do remember. The last time you gave one-word answers to that guy at Simon's party. He mumbled the word 'weird' as he walked away and found his next victim," she giggles. It was as bad as it sounds. I made a complete idiot of myself. Think watermelon moment in Dirty Dancing, but ten times worse.

"My point exactly. And I am also too busy at the moment to date." I try to close down this conversation as there is just no point in it. It is not that I don't want to date. In fact, I am craving to have someone I can trust, share my life with, and with whom I feel comfortable to show my passionate side. But to get there, a guy has to get past the wall I have put up around me. A wall created by past rejections and heartache. And with my looks or, more, the lack of any good looks, no guy finds it worth investing the effort.

"No time," Christina laughs out loud. The bell above the door behind me announces a new customer.

"What are you busy with? Reading steamy romance novels and maxing out the batteries of your vibrator? That doesn't count," Christina adds whilst looking behind me at whomever had just entered the shop. My cheeks turn red, and I give her an angry look. The customer must have heard her. I should just disappear to the backroom, but something makes me turn around. My already red face turns a few shades darker when I face two guys. Two incredibly gorgeous guys. I don't know the shorter one of the two. But the taller, and more handsome one, who grins at me with a cocky smile, is Alex. Alex Harris. We attended the local Chamber of Commerce meeting earlier this month, and I have fantasised about him ever since. Not that I would admit it. We hadn't been introduced, but he was sitting a few chairs away from me, and I couldn't take my eyes off him.

"Don't you agree, gentlemen?" Christina asks them with a serious face but humour in her voice. The shorter guy moves backwards, staring at Christina with panic in his eyes.

"You deal with this," he mumbles to Alex before backing out of the shop. I try to follow his example and move towards the backroom, but Christina cunningly positions herself in the doorway. So unless I am prepared to create a scene and push her aside, there is nowhere to go.

"I agree with your friend. You should definitely go on a date with me and give your vibrator a break." He chuckles and takes another step towards me. Christina laughs, but I am just frozen. He finally notices my discomfort. He stops a meter away from me, wipes the smile from his face, and clears his throat.

Chapter 3

Alex

Well done, you idiot. You made her feel uncomfortable. I am annoyed with myself. I should have seen from the way her cheeks were bright red that the whole situation was uncomfortable for her. But I couldn't help myself. She looked so adorable with her big blue eyes and bright red cheeks. She is wearing baggy dark clothes, but her top has a V neckline, giving me a glimpse of her ample tits. I'd like to strip her clothes away and see what else she is hiding under that T-Shirt. Her face seems to be make up free, and her hair is piled up on top of her head, with some loose streaks framing her face. She is a true natural beauty. I just had to get closer to her until the look on her face made me stop.

Now vulnerability is radiating off her, and I have a distinct feeling that she doesn't trust easily.

"My name is Alex Harris. I'm from the Fellside Mountain Rescue Volunteers or FMR, and I wanted to ask if you could put one of our collection boxes up in your shop." I hold up the little mountain-shaped box and rattle it with my left hand, extending my right one in a greeting. I hope this will allow her to relax a little and ideally erase the memory of my cocky behaviour earlier. Many women would have liked the flirtation, but she clearly felt uneasy, which is the last thing I wanted.

I smile at her, and something crosses her face. It almost looks like disappointment. I wonder what this is about. She looks at my hand, back at me and then my hand again before she briefly shakes it and replies, "Sure, put it next to the till," before attempting to dash to the door her friend is blocking. I softly grab her arm and turn her back to me

"And you are?" I ask. She stares at me for a moment and then whispers:

"Emma."

"In case you didn't get that 'cause you don't have the hearing of a dog, her name is Emma, and I am her best friend, Christina," the dark haired girl behind the till announces loudly. I chuckle as Emma pulls away from me and hisses, "Ex friend," in Christina's direction. I immediately miss the connection and wish I could hold her again.

"I take it you are Estelle's granddaughter. My grandmother is friends with her." I am not sure why I am even saying this other than to make it clear that I am not a complete creep despite my earlier comments. Emma looks at me curiously and nods.

"So, Alex, where can we meet the local guys?" Christina enquires. The thought of Emma meeting someone else rather than being in my arms doesn't sit well. *What has come over me?* I have no right to be this possessive.

"The Unicorn is tucked away behind the market cross, so tourists usually don't find it. That's where most of the village tends to get together," I explain, trying to sound casual.

"Excellent. Does your timid friend also go there?" she asks, and I can see a faint blush coating her cheeks. *Interesting!* I make a mental note to find out if Phil could potentially be interested in Christina. Under no circumstances can I tell him that she is after him because he will just end up hiding. But I can make sure that their paths keep crossing. And it would mean that I get more opportunities with Emma as well. It's a win-win situation.

"Phil and I will be there this afternoon to watch the rugby. You should come. We can introduce you to some other folk here in the village."

"Excellent, we will be there after the shop closes!" Christina's acceptance of my invitation has Emma snap her head in her friend's direction and give her an evil look.

"Great, I'll see you there," I say to Christina before giving Emma another smile and turning to leave the shop. I don't really want to leave. But at least now I know I will see her again soon, which fills me with a warm feeling.

Chapter 4

Emma

"Honestly, woman! That guy was gorgeous and totally into you. And you just stood there and stared at him." Christina rolls her eyes at me. Leaning against the door frame with her hands crossed in front of her, she stares me down.

"No, he wasn't. He didn't even remember me from the Chamber meeting. Alex was just friendly, like everyone else in this village," I reply. I have learned the hard way that guys like him don't go for me. They can get any woman, and they want girly, bubbly and hot. I am frumpy and usually quieter and more reserved than a church mouse. At least until I get to know someone better. I have a passionate, geeky and joyful side. I can get enthusiastic about the weirdest things. But that's not something I share easily. More often than not, when I have shown this side in the past, people told me how ridiculous I am, foremost my mother. The consensus was that I needed to grow up and behave like an adult.

"I think you are wrong." Christina pulls me out of my thoughts. "He was definitely flirting. But I guess, given that I haven't seen you even so much look in the direction of a guy, let alone flirt with one, you might be forgiven for not recognising the signs."

I just roll my eyes in response. She is right that I am a notoriously lousy flirter, but that isn't the issue here. I know men, and I know which men I can get. And Alex isn't in that category.

"Well, we will see later at the pub." Christina grins.

"Wait, what? I am not going to the pub!"

"Yes, you are."

"No, I am not," I reply stubbornly.

"Yes, you are. Otherwise, I'll make you give the presentation at the next Chamber of Commerce meeting," she declares triumphantly.

My stomach drops. Like most shops, we are part of the local Chamber of Commerce networking group. As we are new to the village, they have asked us to present our plans for the shop for the next twelve months and any ideas we have for the community. I hate presentations. I hate being the centre of attention.

Hearing her threat, I know she is not joking. She will refuse to go if I don't give in. She takes our business seriously, but she knows missing the presentation will be embarrassing but not damaging to the company. She also knows I don't share her casual approach to embarrassment and would be left with no alternative but to fill in for her. She knows me way too well.

"Fine, I'll come to the pub," I sigh, and immediately butterflies fill my tummy. Seeing Alex again fills me with dread, but it still feels like the lesser of two evils.

Christina grins, basking in her victory, and returns to the shop floor. But not before shouting, "We leave straight after the shop closes, so don't dawdle."

I look at the half-finished bouquet in my hand. I have lost every inspiration on how to finish it. The only thing on my mind is ensuring I will not make a fool of myself in front of Alex. I can't just sit there like a mute all afternoon, but I have no clue how to keep a casual conversation going with a guy like him either. *Argh*, I am a hopeless case.

Way too soon, Christina reappears in the door and announces that she has closed the shop

"Let's go," she spurs me on. When she sees me attempting to protest, she adds, "And don't even think about coming up with some stupid excuse or stall tactics." *Yup, she definitely knows me too well*. I huff and slowly move the remaining flowers back into the cooler.

"Let's go to your cottage first," Christina says as I lock up the shop's back entrance.

"Why?"

"Because we will put you in some clothes that show off your assets." She points at my boobs and hips.

"There is nothing to show off, and I look good enough for a pub," I reply, but Christina is not accepting this. She snatches my keys out of my hand, opens my flat door next to the shop's back entrance and disappears into my house before I can protest. She really is a very frustrating friend.

By the time I make it to my bedroom on the first floor, she has already emptied half of my wardrobe on my bed.

"What do you think you are doing?" I screech angrily.

"Something in there must have a shape other than a potato sack. Surely you have something form-fitting..." Christina calls out as she reaches deeper into the back of my wardrobe.

I look at the pile of clothes on my bed. They are mainly black and shapeless, helping me hide my big arse and breasts.

"Aha!" Christina calls out and holds up a pale blue top with navy coloured flowers. It has a plunging sweetheart neckline and a soft belt helping to cinch it in at the waist.

"That's for a wedding," I exclaim, "I can't wear that to a village pub."

"Of course you can! Dress it down with a pair of jeans and canvas shoes, and you are pub ready," she grins. She has a determined look on her face, and I know better than to argue with her 'cause I will lose the argument. I am tired, and I just don't have the energy.

"Fine, but it is your fault if I look ridiculous," I growl angrily. But Christina just jumps excitingly and giggles.

I go to the bathroom and put on the clothes. I have to admit, it doesn't look awful. I still think I am overdressed for the pub, but nobody can fight Christina if she has put her mind to something. With another sigh, I put my hair in a messy bun and put on some mascara.

"Let's get this over and done with," I say. Christina looks at me and smiles softly.

"You look amazing. Alex will not know what hit him."

I roll my eyes at her again and grab my phone and bank card. The pub is just down the road, so there is no need to bring more than that with me.

Chapter 5

Alex

"Oh, come on!" Phil exclaims next to me in frustration. England just lost another scrum and are hopelessly behind. This is not the start to the Six Nations Cup we had been hoping for.

"I need another pint. What about you?" I ask whilst getting up from the table. He just nods and then returns his focus to the TV. I grab the two empty glasses from the table. Martin, the pub owner, is also watching the rugby. He pulls his focus from the screen as I step up to the bar.

"Two Oatmeal Stout," I order. Phil and I both prefer local brews over the more common beer brands. Martin nods, grabs the empty glasses I have placed on the bar and deposits them in the dishwasher before pulling clean ones from the shelf.

A sudden draft comes from behind me, telling me that someone has entered the pub. I turn to see who it is—it is a small village, and most likely, it is someone who I know. My breath hitches when Emma enters the pub. She has changed her clothes, and the transformation is mouth-watering. When I thought before that she looked cute, she now just looks absolutely delicious. Her shirt shows off her cleavage, exposing creamy soft skin on top of her tits. The top is cinched at the waist with a belt, showing off the curve of her hips and arse, conjuring up images of me digging my fingers into her soft hips as I push into her.

When she looks up and locks eyes with me, I see a blush colouring her cheeks, and she self-consciously pulls her top a little lower in the back to cover her arse. My mouth goes dry, but a big grin spreads on my cheeks.

"You came," I say to her and Christina, but my eyes are locked on Emma. She tries to fade into the background behind her friend. Christina looks at her disapprovingly before replying to me.

"It was a herculean effort, but I got her here." Emma's cheeks turn even redder, making me hope that the attraction is not one-sided, although it could still be a matter of her just being very shy.

"Well, in that case, what drink can I buy you as a thank you for getting her here?" I ask Christina before winking at Emma. Emma's eyes go wide. Does she not see how attracted I am to her? Maybe I do have to flirt a little harder.

"I'll take what you have," Christina orders, then skips to the table where Phil sits and plonks herself down next to him, leaving a petrified Emma standing in front of me. I take a small step closer and tuck a streak of hair that has come loose behind her ear.

"How about you?" I ask softly. I am so close I can see some little specs of green in her ice-blue eyes.

"Pint of lemonade," she says, her voice almost a whisper. "But I can pay," she adds and holds out her bank card. I put my hand on her arm.

"Nope, this one is on me," I say before turning to Martin and adding the two drinks to my order. Emma stays rooted to the spot, seemingly unsure of what to do.

"Why don't you take mine and Phil's pints to the table, and I bring the other two drinks?" I suggest. She nods and grabs the two pints. Her hands seem to shake a little, but she manages to grip the glasses firmly and carries them to our friends without spillage. I glance at the table whilst Martin swipes my card, and I see Phil stiffly answering a question from Christina. He looks a little like a deer in headlights. I chuckle. This is going to be an interesting afternoon.

When I return to the table, I sit down next to Emma. Christina has taken my chair, so the options are limited. I can't see the TV from my new seat, but the game sucks anyway, and now that Emma is here, I won't be able to focus on anything else than her.

Emma has the fingers of both of her hands around the pint of lemonade. She seems to find comfort by holding onto her drink.

"So how does Fellside compare to London?" I ask her and give her a smile. I hope it is a comforting smile and not a creepy one. She lifts her gaze from the glass in front of her and looks at me from under her eyelashes. She probably doesn't even realise how seductive that looks.

"It's great. I hated London," she says softly.

"I have been to London a few times, and to be honest, I hate it too. Too busy," I agree. "Have you had a chance to explore the area much?" I try to get her to say more.

"No," she replies quietly, but then adds, "But last week, I went for a walk on a path that starts behind the mill and got lost. And I came across this absolutely stunning little waterfall. Not the big one tourists go to—this one is in a little side valley and drops into a pool surrounded by a stunning little meadow. It was so peaceful there. I hope I can find it again." Her face lights up whilst telling me about her little adventure.

"That's the Devil's Child," I explain and pull my phone out of my pocket. I scroll through my pictures until I come to one of the waterfall she described, and show her.

"Yes, that's it. That's the one," she exclaims, joyful. This is a different Emma. She radiates happiness, and I don't know why she hides this from the world.

"Look, Christina, that's the waterfall I told you about. Alex knows it." She hands Christina my phone with a big smile.

"Well, maybe you can take her there one day, Alex. She desperately wants to go back," her friend says with a mischievous look on her face. Emma stiffens next to me.

"No, that's not necessary. Now that I know what it is called, I can just look it up," she says quietly.

"I would love to take you," I reply and take my phone from Christina.

"Why?" asks Emma harshly. Realising her tone, she shrinks back into herself.

I look into her eyes, "I would like to spend more time with you."

"Why?" she asks again.

"Because you are beautiful. You amaze me. And I would love to get to know you more," I reply bluntly.

"I—" She pauses, seemingly unsure what to say. "I am not interested. Sorry. Thanks for the drink, but I think I need to go," she blurts out, stands up, and disappears before either one of us can react.

"Well, looks like my friend is even weirder than yours," Christina says, exasperated, pointing at Phil. He just gives us a blank look like he doesn't know what she is talking about. "Thanks for the drink, Alex. I should go and check she is okay." She reaches for her bag, but she turns to me before leaving. "Are you really interested in her?"

"More than you can imagine," I reply.

"Then don't give up. A lot of people in her past have treated her like shit. They told her she was not good enough, that she was not what anyone would like in their life. What she never had was anyone fighting for her. If you are serious about wanting to get to know her, you will have to be patient and persistent. But believe me, she is worth it. She is an amazing person." Christina is showing for the first time a more serious side, and I appreciate her advice. I nod in acknowledgement. It was good to know that her friend was rooting for us.

Christina taps Phil on his head and says, "See you soon, Bambi," and then struts out of the pub.

Chapter 6

Emma

I am such an idiot. Why do I behave like this? Why? Why can I not shut up the voice in my head telling me that I am not worth it and that I just imagine things?

"Emma, wait." I hear Christina behind me. I stop and turn around. The look on her face tells me that my behaviour was as ridiculous as I thought.

"What the heck was that?" she asks.

"I don't know. He asked me out, and I panicked. I—" But I don't finish the sentence. I can't explain the irrational fear this has caused in me.

"Why? You like him and his asking you out is proof of my earlier argument that he is interested. What is going on?" She clearly doesn't understand my reaction, but she also knows me well enough to see the fear in my eyes.

"Who says he is interested? He could just have other motives."

Christina raises her eyebrows at me.

"Do you hold any state secrets he could be after?" she asks. I know that this all sounds ridiculous.

"Listen, he only had eyes for you the whole time we were there. If you don't trust yourself with what you can see with your own eyes, then trust me." She holds me and locks eyes with me. "I tell you, as a friend, he is interested."

"I doubt he still is after my behaviour just now."

"Wrong again, my friend."

"This will make me sound pathetic, but even if he is, I have no clue how to deal with this. My insecurities are not something I can switch off. And when he looks at me and smiles, I freeze and don't know what to do anymore because I feel like I'm on the edge of an abyss, and if I'll take another step, I will fall." I want to give this a chance, I want to give him a chance and see if Christina is correct, but I also want to hide away and protect myself from heartbreak. You would think that I should find it easier to get over heartache, having been hurt as often as I have. Truth be told, I am not sure if I can take any more pain. I have a tendency to throw myself into every situation with my whole heart. I am not used to just taking it easy and seeing where it leads. It takes a lot for me to open up to someone. So naturally, if I trust someone that much, I have to be in it completely. And if it ends in tears, it hurts. Things going badly with Alex would hurt a lot. And I am sick and tired of the pain. Running seems to be the safest option.

"Listen to me." Christina pulls me from my thoughts. "I know you are scared, and I get it. But please trust me, this could be good. And you deserve to be happy for once. Give him a chance."

"Well, I turned him down, so that's that."

"I would say you can just go back and accept." Christina giggles when she sees my horrified expression. "But let's face it: it is you," she declares. I hang my head. I am brave in many things but never in matters of my heart.

"Don't worry. I don't think you have seen the last of him," she finally says as we arrive at my cottage.

I shrug and unlock my door. "Do you want to come in?"

"Nope, I'm heading home, taking a bath and doing some online shopping. I need a new outfit that knocks Bambi's socks off."

"Who the heck is Bambi?" I ask.

"Phil, Alex's friend. He is cute but timid like Bambi." She giggles. "He is like a male version of you, but I am determined." She grins.

"Well, then, happy hunting," I laugh and wave as she walks off.

I close my door and lean against it. Why can I not be a bit more like Christina?

***

24

I hate Mondays. Monday is when I place the orders for the week, which means a lot of counting. I hear the bell above the entrance door chime. Christina is delivering some flowers, so I shout to the front, "I will be there in a moment," before putting my clipboard down and closing the walk-in fridge. I see Charlotte standing at the counter with a box in her hand. Charlotte moved to the Lakes from London, like me. She is a little older, but we clicked immediately when we first met and have developed a friendship since. Charlotte has been through a nasty divorce where her husband left her for a much younger woman, but she has used her anger, transformed it into creative energy, and produced some stunning artwork. She now owns a gallery in town where she not only sells artwork from local artists but also her own. Her gallery is a popular hot spot for tourists.

When I met her for the first time, I fell in love with the vases and pots she crafted, and I proposed I could also display some for her and sell them with my flowers.

"Hey, Charlotte," I greet her.

"Hey. New stock for you." She points to the box. I peek inside and pull out three beautiful vases. I also see some smaller objects wrapped in newspaper at the bottom of the box.

"What is this?" I ask her curiously.

"These are new. They are statues of lovers in different positions embracing each other," she explains, and when she sees me blushing, adds with a laugh, "No, not that kind of an embrace. Just a normal hug." I giggle and pull one of the small parcels out of the box. I carefully unwrap it from the newspaper.

"Oh my god, this is amazing," I exclaim. I hold in my hand the most delicate little statue, with the silhouette of two people hugging.

"I made them from clay and painted them with a colour that looks like the stone formations in Cappadocia. It gives them the appearance of being carved out of stone." She smiles proudly.

"It does," I agree and look around the shop to work out where to best put them.

"You know what, I have wanted to put a shelf on this naked wall for a while and was thinking of displaying plants, but it would be a much better place for these ones. People will love them. How much do I sell them for?" Excitement is apparent in my voice. They really are amazing.

She tells me the retail price, and even with the twenty percent commission I put on top of her products, they are still within the budget of any regular tourist.

"Do you have more?" I ask her. "If I want them displayed on the shelf and a few in the window so people passing can see them, I need at least twelve to fifteen."

"I wasn't sure if you would like them, so I only brought three, but I can have another ten over to you by tomorrow," she suggests. I nod and carefully put the little figurine back in its box.

We both catch up on each other's lives, but not that much has happened. Once Charlotte leaves, I dig out the flatpack shelf I bought months ago and bring it to the shop floor. The wall to the left of the entrance is painted in pale mint green, but otherwise, it is blank. The flatpack is a set of three floating shelves in grass green. The fixture holding them up will be concealed inside the wood, making it look like it is floating. It will be perfect for the statues. I am considering painting the area immediately behind the shelf in the same green, creating the visual of three little alcoves. The ideal place to display the little figurines.

I grab the first of the three shelves and read the instructions. *Sounds easy enough.* I put the ladder next to the wall to put the highest one up first. I will place them at slightly different heights spread out along the wall.

It takes me about 45 minutes and a lot of swearing to assemble the first shelf. I had to download an app to act as a water scale but looking at my handiwork, I am unsure how accurate the app is. It doesn't really look level. I grab a little glass sphere we keep as a paperweight on the counter and position it on the shelf. As I let go, it rolls to the right and off the shelf, and I catch it mid-air.

"I don't think that is straight." I hear behind me. I don't need to turn around to know it is Alex. I would recognise his voice out of a crowd.

"Ah, no. Hi." I stumble and blush when locking eyes with him. He is leaning against the doorframe, arms crossed in front of his chest. He is wearing cargo trousers and a tight black t-shirt with the FMR team logo on it. I love a man in cargo trousers, especially if he has the right bum. And he has a mighty fine arse.

"Looks like you could do with my services," he declares with a cheeky smile. I can feel panic rising in me. Alex's flirty words cause a familiar anxiety. I swallow hard. He takes a step closer and inspects the shelf.

"This won't hold for long," he nods towards the shelf.

"It's just fine," I explain and hold onto the shelf to stop myself from running. A loud crack fills the silence. Next thing I know, the piece of wood is no longer fixed to the wall; instead, I am holding it in my hand.

"Would you like to retract your last statement?"

"I just need to tighten the screws more." I try to argue my case.

"Or you need to use plasterboard fixtures because this is just a plasterboard." He knocks against the wall, and the noise is hollow. "Let me fix it for you."

"Women can do this kind of work," I declare stubbornly. He laughs. *What the heck?*

"I know women can, but you clearly can't. I am a carpenter and although I don't usually put up flatpacks, assembling shelves is part of my job description. What are you trying to do with them?" he asks, not giving me a chance to push back.

I look at him for a long moment before taking a deep breath. I explain what I had been planning. Weirdly his presence makes me nervous but also makes me feel protected and calm.

He carefully lifts one of the little statues from the counter and looks at it curiously.

"I like your idea, but I think it would look a lot nicer and in line with the shop's style if we put dark brown oak shelves and paint the area behind it moss green." He looks at me, excitement sparkling in his eyes. He is right, dark oak shelves would be amazing, but they are not affordable. Flatpack is as far as our money stretches.

"Maybe, but that is out of my budget," I reply, acting like I am not getting excited by his vision.

He shrugs. "Well, why don't I get my tools and fix these for you?"

"That's not—" I am about to decline again when he steps closer and puts a finger on my lips. He is so close that I can feel his heat and smell his scent. Woodsy and manly. He locks eyes with me and says softly, "Just let me help you. That's what we do here. We help each other. I don't expect anything in return." My heart is racing, and I am lost in his eyes. How can I say no to this? I find it difficult to breathe at the moment. Forming words is not on the cards, so I just nod.

"You close at four, correct?" he asks, and I nod again. "Great, I will be back then."

"Okay," I whisper and attempt to smile when he gives me a big grin and walks out of the shop. On his way out, he greets Christina, who had been standing at the entrance watching us. She acknowledges him and then turns her eyes to me.

"Okay, what did I miss?" she asks after the door closes behind him. She walks to the counter where our till sits and deposits the tip she received for the delivery in the tip jar. As we both co-own the shop, we have gotten into the habit of dropping tips into the tip jar and using that money for lunches or similar treats.

"Nothing. Charlotte dropped off these cute pieces of art." I show her. "And I thought I could finally put up the shelves and we could display them there. Alex thinks my shelf-building skills are lacking."

Christina laughs.

"Well, I would say he is right." She points to the broken shelf on the floor.

"I could have sorted it, but he insisted on fixing it."

"Fixing it, ha! Going by the intimate scene I found you both in, he wants to do much more than just fix your shelf." She wiggles her eyebrows.

"There was nothing intimate," I reply, but I know she won't buy this bullshit. Hell, even I don't believe it anymore. The moment we shared was intimate and had my insides tied up in a ball.

"You tell yourself that." She chuckles as the phone on the counter rings. "In any case, I am finishing early today, so you have no choice but to stay and wait for Alex. No hiding this time." I want to protest, but she holds up a finger to silence me and answers the phone. She knows me too well. With her around, there would be the potential that I would panic again and try to escape before Alex's return. But I can't leave the shop if she is not here. Damn, she has me there.

Chapter 7

Alex

I park my car behind the store and unload some of the materials from the back of my Range Rover. I'm currently working on a big farm house, and they have a lot of bespoke oak furniture. I had some offcuts left over that are just the right size for the shelves Emma wants. I cut and stained them when I returned to the workshop. They now look dark brown and weathered. I also brought moss green paint with me. The whole job should not take me longer than an hour.

I walk into the shop, and the doorbell announces my arrival.

"I will be there in a moment," Emma shouts from the back. There isn't the usual nervousness in her voice, which I assume is because she doesn't know it is me yet. If I haven't said it before, I find her nervousness adorable.

"No rush, I'll just bring my materials in," I shout back. Nothing. I chuckle. She is probably sitting in the back trying to devise a plan to avoid me. I leave her to her plotting, knowing with no sign of Christina in the shop, she has no option but to hang around.

I grab the rest of the materials, my toolkit and the paint from my car. Just as I close the door, Emma finally appears, giving me a cautious smile.

"Hey," I grin at her. She has a little streak of dirt on her cheek, and I can't help myself but reach out, cup her face and wipe the dirt off her cheek with my thumb.

In her haste to escape my touch, she doesn't remember the buckets with flowers behind her and promptly stumbles over one. She loses her footing and crash-lands on the floor but not before knocking four more buckets over. Water and flowers spill everywhere.

"Oh, shit, are you okay?" I ask. I move an arm around her waist and pull her up. Her hands land on my chest, and I can smell something fruity. Maybe her shampoo? This is the

30

closest I have ever been to her, and it feels right. She feels perfect in my arms. I shift, keeping one hand on her lower back, and with my other hand, I push a streak of hair behind her ear. My fingers linger on her skin, and the urge to kiss her takes over. My dick starts to strain against my zipper. She says nothing and just stares at me, her cheeks blushing crimson.

"I should start putting the shelves up," I try to break the tension and point towards the wall. I have sworn myself to take it slow, but she is making it very difficult.

"Okay," she whispers.

"Are you alright?" I ask again, concerned.

"Wet," she replies. I swallow a groan cause this innocent word brings visions of a different kind of wetness between her legs to my mind.

"Do you need me to give you a hand with this?" I point at the water-flower bombsite on the floor.

"No…no," she stutters and walks to the backroom before returning with a mop and bucket.

After locking the shop door, we work quietly. Emma is cleaning up the mess on the floor and trying to save some of the flowers. I am measuring out the area to paint and the holes for the shelf fittings. It doesn't take long to find the right spot to set the plasterboard fixings so I can secure the screws. Thank god this job is easy 'cause it is damn hard to focus on the work at hand. I'm too aware of her presence. She felt so right in my arms. It took all of my willpower to stop me from kissing her, but I know this would have been the worst thing I could have done. She spooks easier than a mouse, and I know I must move slowly, let her get comfortable and see that she can trust me. But there was a glimmer of hope. I saw a hint of desire in her eyes, a promise of fire and passion. And she didn't move away from me for the first time since we met a few days ago.

I put the last screw in place and check that the shelves are level. They are in perfect balance. I turn around and notice that Emma has finished cleaning. She is sitting on a little stool behind the till, elbows on the counter and her chin in her hands, looking at my crotch with a dreamy look. Well, a minute ago, it would have been the spot where my arse was. I clear my throat.

Emma shoots up like she has been hit by lightning and, in the process, knocks over a jar of pens. *Gotcha!* I grin to myself. She blushes deep red and bends down to pick up the pens. However, she underestimates the distance to the counter and crashes her forehead on the wooden edge.

"Ouch," she exclaims, straightens and holds her head.

"Are you okay?" I ask for the third time this afternoon. I take a step towards her, remove her hand from her face and carefully inspect the area where her head had made contact with the counter. Emma doesn't move. Our eyes are locked whilst I softly stroke the patch of skin. An incredible need to kiss her fills me. It is impossible that she doesn't feel the pull between us. It wouldn't take much for me to close the narrow gap and melt my lips to hers. But I can't.

I take a deep breath and break our eye contact. I focus my eyes on her forehead, where a small red bruise is forming. She winces when I put a little pressure on that particular spot.

"You are going to get a bump. But the skin is not broken." She looks at me with desire in her eyes. Her breathing is speeding up, and she nervously bites her bottom lip. With the fingers of my left hand, I slowly trace a path from her forehead over her cheek to her lips. I free her lip from the grasp of her teeth. My thumb swipes from the left corner to the right corner of her mouth. *I need to kiss her.* I slowly move closer. My brain is screaming that I should stop. I should step away before I do something that she doesn't want. Just as I am about to listen to my brain, her fingers grab hold of my T-shirt. This simple gesture is enough for me to know she wants this too.

I push Emma against the nearest wall, aligning our bodies. My eyes are locked on hers. My right hand moves to her hip and holds her in place. She lowers her gaze but doesn't move. I brush a loose lock of hair out of her face before lifting her chin until her eyes meet mine again. Her breath hitches.

Slowly, I lean in closer, so close that I can feel her ragged breath fanning over my face. And then I wait. I can see the desire in her eyes, but I don't cross the last line. I need to know that she really wants this. I want her to take the final step. I would wait for a thousand years for her to take what she needs. But I only have to wait for a few seconds.

Her eyelids drop shut, and she lifts her head higher with her lips aiming for mine. That's good enough for me. I meet her head-on and close the final gap. Our warm lips connect, and a fire burns through my body. I pull her closer. Emma moves one of her hands to my chest and, with the other, cups my cheek. A little moan escapes her throat when I softly bite her bottom lip. I urge her to give me access to her warm mouth, and she willingly invites me in. The kiss turns from urgent to sensual and passionate. My hard cock is pressed against her front, yet I want to get even closer. I want to strip her out of her clothes and melt into her. My lips travel from her mouth to her ear. I kiss a trail down her throat to her collarbone before moving back to her mouth for another deep and passionate kiss.

My heart is beating like a jackhammer when our tongues meet, and my dick is straining painfully against the zipper of my jeans. He definitely wants to come out and play. I feel a need to touch her everywhere. I need to feel her skin under my fingers. All I can taste and smell is her, and I am instantly addicted. In our frantic attempt to get closer, we step too far to the left, and I accidentally push my toolbox over. The loud crash brings us back to reality.

She stares at me, her breath still laboured. I softly peck her lips one more time and then take a step back. I have to muster all my willpower to get me to move away, but I know it is the right thing to do.

"Let me take you out on a date." I ask, hoping for a different answer than she gave me at the pub. I can see the conflict in her eyes, fear, desire and something much deeper that I can't identify. She lowers her gaze again, but I put my finger under her chin and lift it up so she can't avoid me.

"Just dinner, that's all it is. No pressure."

"For you, it might just be dinner. It will be an anxiety-filled evening of me worrying I will embarrass myself, say something stupid or jump too quickly to conclusions. Just to name a few of my fears." She looks sad when she says this. I have a feeling she has been fighting an inner battle for a while, and fear usually wins.

"Emma, everything you have done so far that you felt embarrassed by, I just found adorably quirky. I don't play games. I am interested in you and want to get to know you better."

"You can do so much better than me."

"We need to work on your self-confidence." I chuckle.

"Alex, I know what I look like. I have a mirror. You will also soon find out that I am a weirdo."

"Does this mean you will go out with me?" I am going to ignore her self-criticism for now, as I can feel that I am close to victory. She slowly nods. I can't stop the big grin lighting up my face.

"We should wrap up here, and then I'll take you for dinner," I announce.

"Today?" she asks with a shocked look on her face.

"Can't risk you skipping town," I smirk, and she blushes.

Chapter 8

Emma

Once we finish the work in the shop, Alex loads his tools in his car. The shelves with the dark green background look fantastic, and I am glad he ignored my protests when I insisted he sticks to my flatpack shelves. I can't afford to pay for the work he has done, but he assured me there would be no cost. I am usually not one to accept charity, but I can't wait to get the rest of the figurines delivered from Charlotte tomorrow because the shelves look so good.

I grab my keys and walk to the door to lock up. The minute I put the key in the lock, my heart starts beating like crazy. I had pushed the thought of dinner with Alex to the back of my mind, but now there is no avoiding it.

"Ready?" I hear Alex's smooth voice from behind me. I take a deep breath, turn around and nod.

"But I should quick pop home for my wallet and change my clothes," I say, insecurity apparent in my voice. Alex takes my hand and links our fingers.

"You look perfect, and dinner is on me." He softly drags me towards the high street. "Do you like Arabic food?"

"Yes," I reply with excitement. I have heard that a new Lebanese restaurant has opened in Fellside. A brave decision from the owner, given that small villages in England are not known to embrace multicultural trends. Still, the villagers are all cuckoo about the new place.

"I fell in love with Arabic food when I travelled to Beirut," I explain.

"You have been to Lebanon?" he asks with admiration in his voice.

"Yup, I've travelled to many countries in the Middle East. I think I got my travel bug from my Nana. I love the Middle Eastern culture, and Lebanon has definitely become my favourite country in the region." I go on to talk about the caves

I visited, the Beirut culture and the crusaders' castles I had seen. I talk so much that by the time I finish my monologue, we are seated at the restaurant. Alex just looks at me and I suddenly am aware that he hasn't said a word since we left my shop.

"I am so sorry," I whisper. I'm doing it again. I should know by now that people are not interested to hear all about my boring trips. My friends have made that abundantly clear.

"Why are you apologising?" Alex asks and then opens his menu.

"Because I know this is very boring. You should have stopped me." Alex looks up from the menu and locks eyes with me. Ashamed, I look away and open my own menu.

"Emms, please look at me," he calls me out. I sigh but do as he asks. I like that he calls me Emms. Only my Nana usually calls me that.

"I want to hear these things. You clearly love travelling and exploring places, and everything you told me just now makes me want to go to Lebanon. There was nothing boring. Anyone who told you otherwise is an idiot. I want to hear about the things you enjoy and the things you don't like. I told you I want to get to know you."

I giggle, and when he raises an eyebrow curiously, I explain, "You basically just called my mother an idiot."

"Your mother told you that you are boring?"

"That's one of the many things she feels the need to criticise me on." I shrug my shoulders. Before Alex can reply, the waiter interrupts us.

"As-salaam aleikum, welcome to Jann. What can I get you?" he greets us with a friendly smile. Alex points at me.

"Emma is the expert on Arabic food, so I'll let her order for us." I blush, having the attention drawn to me.

"I am not an expert," I whisper.

"She has travelled the Middle East, so she definitely knows more than me," he explains to the waiter and then adds to me, "Order. I fully trust you." The waiter notices my insecurity and gives me an encouraging smile.

"Can we get two lemon-mint, please? Can we also get a mezza, some Kousa Mahshi, Fattoush, Shish Taouk, some falafel and some Kibbeh? And if he doesn't like what I have ordered, add some fries," I rattle off our order and smile, forgetting for one moment my nerves. The waiter writes it all down and says, "Definitely a small expert," and winks at me.

I can feel the heat intensify in my cheeks and look at Alex, who eyes me with a fascinated expression on his face.

"I don't really know what you ordered but going by the look on your face, we are in for a treat." I blush even more. *Argh*! I hate that I blush all the time.

"They will bring it all at once, and you pick out the bits you like. I hope you don't mind that I didn't order you your own dish…" I ask, worry spreading through me.

"Not at all," he assures and gives me a big smile. He reaches out and grabs my hand. His thumb is casually stroking the back of it. This simple gesture helps me to relax a little. He asks me more questions about my travels, and after some initial hesitation, I am more than happy to talk about my adventures. I have him in stitches when I tell him about my many mishaps, like when I took an involuntary mud bath on a hike in Scotland. He follows my stories with his own funny anecdotes. Although he hasn't travelled much abroad, he has explored the English islands extensively and has me laughing in no time.

His eyes light up when the waiters fill our table with delicious dishes. Some of the other diners give us questioning looks, however, Alex's enthusiasm distracts me from caring about other people's opinions. He tries all the dishes and then keeps going back to his favourites. After the meal, the waiter brings us complimentary baklava, and Alex insists on feeding me. He goes so far as to hold the plate out of reach and makes me take a bite from the small pastry in his hand. His fingers swipe across my lips when I take a bite, and I almost choke on the delicious sweet. Alex's eyes turn dark. My heart starts racing. He puts the rest of the pastry in his mouth and licks the syrup off his fingers. Unconsciously my tongue licks my lips, mirroring his tongue movement.

When I realise what I am doing, I blush, and luckily I am rescued by the waiter who steps up to our table with our bill. Alex praises the food whilst paying, and I notice that he leaves a generous tip.

"Ready?" he asks me and holds out his hand. I hesitantly put my hand in his, and he immediately locks our fingers. He carefully pulls me from my chair and towards the door. Once outside the restaurant, we slowly walk towards my cottage. I don't know what time it is, but it is already dark. We seem to walk as slowly as possible to make the time together last longer, but Fellside is not big, and it doesn't take long to end up on my doorstep.

"Thank you for dinner," I say and pull my keys from my pocket. I put them in the lock, but Alex's hand lands on mine before I can turn the keys. His other hand grabs hold of my hip and makes me face him. When I shyly look at him, he leans his forehead against mine.

"I had an amazing time," he whispers. "You are an amazing woman." I forget to breath for a moment. I can't remember the last time someone made me feel so good about myself. A warmth spreads through me at his words. His hand cups my chin and slowly lifts it. I close my eyes, and then his lips are on mine.

The kiss starts slower than the one in my shop, but it still holds the same punch. A shiver runs down my back, and I tilt my head. Alex takes this as a sign to deepen the kiss. His tongue seeks entrance to my mouth. A soft moan escapes me, and this seems to break all of Alex's restraints. He presses me up against my door, one hand finding its way to the back of my head, the other to my arse, pulling me closer. My hands snake around his neck, and for once, I don't think, I just feel. My whole body is alert and vibrating with need. I soak up his taste and his smell, and my brain catalogues it for later.

When we break apart for air, I notice that I am shaking, and I am unsure if it is from need or arousal.

"Good night," Alex whispers and then gives me a final chaste kiss. I sigh, turn the key in my lock and step into my house. Before I close the door, I give him a smile.

"Night," I whisper. The look he gives me, full of desire and need, causes me almost to pull him into the house, but of course, I don't. Instead, I slowly close the door. I realise that I feel entirely happy for the first time in my life.

Chapter 9

Alex

It took everything from me to let Emma go. I can't remember the last time I had so much fun on a date. Once she started talking about her travels, she showed a passion for life that captivated me. Her blue eyes sparkled, and her whole aura relaxed and radiated. Listening to her made me want to pack my bags, take her by the hand and explore the world together. Truthfully, aside from a couple of trips to Spain with friends, I usually holiday in the UK. When I was younger, I didn't have the funds to explore the world, and my company kept me busy as I got older. Now I am wondering if I have missed out. But then, it is never too late.

I get into my car and drive the short distance to my house. I take my shoes off at the entrance and walk in just socks to the kitchen. I grab a bottle of beer from the fridge and pull my phone from my pocket. That's when I realise that I am an idiot. We never exchanged numbers. I want to kick myself. I can't even say goodnight or ask her for another date. Annoyed with myself, I go to bed, planning a trip to Emma's shop first thing in the morning.

***

I look at my watch and see it is twelve noon. I got called out to a mountain rescue early this morning: two tourists thought watching the sunrise on the mountain would be a great idea and got lost in the dark on the way to the summit. It didn't take us long to find them and guide them down, but by the time I had finished the report and tidied all the equipment away, ready for the next rescue, it was ten, and I had to get to my workshop to make it to an appointment. Now that the meeting is over, I know I need to see Emma despite being behind on work. Most importantly, I need to ensure she knows I want to see her again.

As I walk past the Cherry Pie bakery, I grab three delicious éclairs and three coffees. Most likely, Christina will be there as well, and it would be rude not to bring her one.

As I enter the shop, I see Christina typing on the computer. She looks up, and a big grin appears on her face. I take it as a good sign that Emma's review of our date was positive. I lift my finger to my lips so she doesn't give me away and point to the backroom, whispering, "Emma?" Christina nods, and I grin. I put a coffee and a pastry on the counter for her, and she whispers, "No need to bribe me." I hold back a chuckle.

As I step into the cool backroom, I see her sitting on the floor. Her hair is up in her usual messy bun, and she wears her trademark jeans and oversized shirt. The memory of our two kisses yesterday floods back in my mind, and I sigh loudly. The noise alerts Emma, and she lifts her gaze. Her face lights up when she sees me, and I just want to lift her up and kiss the hell out of her. But I restrain myself and put the pastries and coffee on the desk along the wall.

"I wanted to bring you breakfast, but I was called to a rescue, so now it is more of an early lunch," I explain.

"You didn't have to."

"Oh, I did. Firstly, I don't have your number and therefore could not send you a good night message or ask you for another date. So, here I am to ask in person," I explain, raising my arms and pointing at myself. "And secondly, I wanted to see you. I needed to see you." She blushes and holds out her hand.

"Give me your phone," she demands. I unlock my Android device and hand it to her. She quickly types her name and number into my phone, and when I hear a vibration from her desk, I know she has sent herself a message, so she has my number as well.

"Problem solved," She exclaims. I shake my head and hold out my hand. She drops my phone in it. I, in turn, put it in my pocket and then hold out my hand again. She looks at me before slowly putting her hand in mine. I pull her up and toward me until her body is pressed against mine. I capture her face in my palms and lean forward.

"Belated good morning," I whisper and then press my lips to her. She doesn't hesitate this time but kisses me back passionately. I invade her mouth with my tongue and feel immediately alive when I taste her. It has only been a few hours, but I missed her. Small moans escape Emma when I deepen the kiss, and she grabs onto my T-shirt to stop me from ending the kiss.

"Emma, do we have—" Christina steps into the backroom. Emma takes a few steps away from me until she is out of reach. Immediately I miss the contact and frown. Christina, on the other hand, has a big grin on her face.

"Sorry to interrupt," she says with a cheeky smile. "I need some sunflowers if we have some. A customer is looking for ten." Emma just nods and steps into the walk-in fridge. A blush covers her cheeks. Despite the cool air of the storage area, when she steps back out, she is still as pink as when she went in.

Christina takes the flowers and grins. "I will be in the front so you can continue—" She makes kissing noises. Emma goes bright read, and I chuckle. I just hope this doesn't spook my woman back behind her wall. *My woman.* I don't know when I have become a caveman, but I like the sound of that.

Once Christina has left the room, Emma avoids my gaze and nervously looks to the floor. I put one hand around her waist and pull her back to me.

"When can I take you out again?" I ask.

"You don't have to," she replies timidly. There she is, my shy, self-conscious Emma.

"I want to. Frankly, if I could, I would kidnap you now, but the rescue has put me behind schedule, so I really need to get back to my workshop."

"If you are busy, it's okay. You can call me some time next week, or—" I don't let her finish. I close her mouth with a kiss and then say:

42

"There is no way I will wait for a week to take you out again. What are you doing on Friday night?"

"Nothing, she has zero plans," shouts Christina from the front. Emma frowns and then pushes the door between the backroom and the shop close.

"I'm free if you really want to meet."

"I do. Do you want to?" I ask. She looks embarrassed but doesn't hesitate and lets me know with a nod that she also wants to see me again. I can't help it, but her admitting that makes me grin like I just won the lottery.

"Okay then, I'll pick you up at seven." I bend forward and steal one last kiss. I want it to be a quick one, but when she opens up to me, my body reacts automatically. I press my hips against hers and slide my hands over her arse. My dick is hard and pressing into her tummy, but I don't care that she can feel how much I want her. As I pull away from her, she sucks my lower lip in her mouth, and I almost lose all my willpower.

"I'll text you later," I say, steal a quick, chaste kiss and leave the backroom.

I wish Christina a good day as I walk past her, and she smiles at me.

"Have a good day too. And say hello to Bambi for me."

"Who?" I ask, utterly confused.

"Phil, your timid friend who looks at me like a deer in headlights. Bambi," she explains. I look at her for a moment and then burst out laughing. Oh, Phil is so going to hear about this.

"I will tell him. He is single, by the way," I explain.

"Duh, he can barely string together a full sentence when a woman is present. Didn't think him to be a ladies' man," she giggles. "But I am not easily dissuaded."

I chuckle again. Poor Phil. He is not going to know what hit him. But I approve. She could be good for him. I give her a thumbs up to show her my support before leaving the shop.

Chapter 10

Emma

"Okay, you so did not tell me the truth about the date yesterday!" Christina accuses me as she storms into the backroom. "You said it was okay," she throws my own understatement back at me, "but there is no way the kiss just now was the first time he kissed you." I look past her to the shop floor, but she shakes her head.

"No customers there, so spill," she demands.

I am tempted to downplay it, but I know it is a lost battle. I can't hold my smile back as I give her more details about our date. Christina listens to me with a smile on her face. But when I finish, cheeks flushed and a grin like the Cheshire cat on my face, she looks at me in earnest.

"How do you feel about this?" she asks carefully. I take a deep breath.

"I am…" I take another deep breath, "I am elated and happy, and it scares me. What if I read this all wrong? What if I am in too deep too quick? He might just consider this as a casual thing. Can I just go with the flow? I don't think so," I blurt out and hide my face in my hands in frustration.

"Listen to me." Christina draws back my attention. "I have seen the way he looks at you. Add that to the things he says to you and the gestures he makes, and this is not a guy who is just interested in casual. When you are together, does it feel right?"

"So right. Like a piece I had been missing all my life is no longer missing. I feel complete and myself with him," I whisper. There is no reply, so I remove my hands from my face and look at Christina. Her face says it all. She truly believes this could be the real deal and is happy for me.

"Trust yourself and trust him. You deserve this," she gives me as parting advice before returning to the shop as the doorbell indicates a customer's arrival.

I'm glad when four o'clock comes round, and I can lock up the shop. At home, I strip off and put on some yoga pants and an oversized T-shirt. I cook some pasta and decide to take a long bath. One of the few things I changed on the cottage when I moved in was to install a large and deep bathtub. Nothing relaxes me as much as taking a bath.

I light a few candles and get undressed whilst the bath fills up. The scent of lemongrass and coconut from the bubble bath I have added to the water fills the room. I am about to step into the tub when my phone vibrates, alerting me to a message. I snatch it from my bedroom and take it to the bathroom. I put it on the little counter next to the bath and step into the hot water. As the soapy water engulfs me, I feel my muscles relax. I settle back, dry my hands and grab the phone. I see the text is from Alex, and a smile automatically lifts the corners of my mouth.

Alex: Did you have a good day?
Me: I did. Did you manage to catch up on work?

God, I really suck at flirting. I could have said something back about how his visit this lunchtime put me in a good mood.

Alex: Nope. My mind kept drifting to you, so I made a couple of mistakes but nothing that I can't catch up on tomorrow.

Say something flirty! Say something witty!

Me: Did you know that distractions can improve creativity?

Great, yes, bore him to death with some ridiculously tedious facts!

Me: Forget I said that. That sounded better in my head.
Alex: Hey, I could do with some creativity. I am trying to come up with an idea for our next date.
Me: Oh, I'm easy.

Alex: Is that so? *winky face*

Fan-fucking-tastic! I want to bang my head against the edge of the tub. Of course, that's not what I had meant, but trust me to phrase it that way.

Me: I mean, I don't need to be wooed.
Alex: I don't mean to woo you. I want to create memories with you we can look back on in years to come and say, "this is how it all started"

Okay, now this was nice. My heart beats faster at the hint that he wants this to be something long-term.

Alex: What are you doing tonight?
Me: I'll probably watch this documentary about black sites in the UK.

Thumbs up to me! That's how to make sure he knows how boring you are.

Alex: Black sites, as in where they pretend laws don't apply and they torture people?
Me: Oh god, no. I meant Dark Sky Sites where the stars are visible because there is hardly any or no man-made light present. There are a few of these sites in the Lake District.
Alex: You like star gazing?
Me: Yes and no. I don't care much about science or the names of the different star constellations. I just like to look at them and feel the might of Mother Nature and how small we all are in comparison. I always wanted to go to one of these sites, but Christina finds it boring, and I don't want to go alone.
Alex: Is the documentary on now? I feel I should look into this.
Me: Nope, in an hour. That's why I decided to take a bath first.
Alex: You are having a bath right now?

I groan. I really didn't need to tell him this.

Me: Yes. *blushing emoji*
Alex: You are killing me.

I sink lower into the water and decide it is time to change the topic.

Emma: What are you doing.

And we are back to dull.

Alex: I was cooking dinner but burned it because you distracted me.
Emma: *Giggling emoji* Well, you texted me. I'll let you go, though, so you can finish your dinner.
Alex: I'll text you again, and Emma...
Alex: I can't wait to see you Friday.

I smile. I type "Me too", then delete it, type it again and delete it again. I am not quite ready to show all my cards.

Emma: Have a good evening.

Chapter 11

Alex

This week has been incredibly slow. I threw myself into work and pulled a few ten-hour days to help me catch up on work and make time move faster until my date with Emma. It is finally Friday, and I can finish at noon, thanks to my overtime. I am driving to my FMR buddy Christopher. His farm is in a narrow valley not far from Fellside. As I stop outside the large farm building, Chris comes out of the stables.

"Are you going to tell me now why you need my truck and access to my field tonight?" he asks instead of greeting me.

"I am creating a memory," I reply cryptically.

"Phil mentioned that you met someone. Has it got to do with her?" he interrogates. I grin, and I don't need to say more. I walk to his truck. He has one of these two-seater pickup trucks so popular in the USA. You won't find many here in the UK, though. Lucky for me, Chris loves American cars.

I see he has washed out the cargo bed as requested to ensure it wasn't dirty.

"And why can't you take your own Range Rover to woo this woman?" he asks. "Your Range has the same amount of power as my truck."

"But it hasn't got a cargo bed," I explain. He raises his eyebrow but doesn't ask further questions. He knows if I don't want to give him more details, it probably is for a reason. Truth be told, I want to surprise Emma, and I want this to be between her and me and not the whole of Fellside to know before she has a chance to experience it. Not that Chris tends to gossip a lot, but things have a way of spreading around the village like wildfire, and I am rather safe than sorry.

"Well, just bring it back to me when you are done. The keys to the Stone Meadow are in the glove box," he explains. I shake his hand and promise to catch up with him and the remaining FMR team sometime next week.

***

The clock on the dashboard of the pick-up truck tells me I am five minutes early. I park in front of the shop rather than at the back next to Emma's cottage. I want this all to be a surprise.

I knock, and my breath hitches when she opens the door. She is wearing skinny jeans showing off her shapely legs and arse and a blue top that hugs her breasts. It is tight at the waist and then flares out. I swallow down a groan. As much as I like her in that top, I really, really would like to see her not wearing it.

She smiles at me insecurely and tugs a little on her shirt.

"I wasn't sure where we would be going. Is this okay?" she asks. I pull Emma into my arms and softly kiss her.

"More than okay. You look beautiful." She blushes and leans her head against my chest. I take a deep breath and softly stroke her back. I could stay like this forever but I also want to show her my surprise.

"Right, do you trust me?" I ask, bringing us back to the moment. She looks at me. Something crosses her face. It might be fear. But she seems to push it back and eventually nods. I hold out a blindfold.

"Would you wear this?" I ask her, nervous she may say no. When I see her fearful face, I add, "Just until we get to our destination. I want it to be a surprise." She takes the blindfold and looks at it.

"Trust me. I would never do anything to harm you," I whisper. She searches my eyes.

"I trust you," she finally declares. Her trust is not easily earned, and we both know this is a big moment. I carefully place the blindfold over her eyes and test that she definitely can't see anything. I guide her around the corner to Chris's truck, open the passenger door and help her in.

"It's about a thirty-minute drive," I say as I take a seat on the driver's side. Emma just nods. I reach out and hold her hand

49

to help her calm down. I occasionally catch her taking a deep breath. She is nervous, but she wants to trust me, and I can only imagine what internal battle she is fighting.

When we finally get to the gate at the area called Stone Meadow, a remote corner on Christopher's farm, I stop the car.

"I will be back in a minute," I explain, but before I can open the door, she grabs my hand.

"Where are you going?" Fear laces her voice.

"I am just unlocking a gate. Trust me." I try to reassure her. She takes a deep breath and lets go of me. I rush to get the gate unlocked and drive us through before locking the gate behind us again. The minute I am back in the car, I reach out for her hand. She visually relaxes. We drive for another five minutes, but eventually, I park the car in the middle of a field.

I help Emma out of the car.

"Don't take the blindfold off," I remind her before opening the tailgate and removing the plastic cover protecting the small mattress. I lay out the duvet and pillows I had on the back seat and put the cooler with the picnic near the car's rear window, which I can open from the outside when sitting on the cargo bed.

"Right, up you go." I lift Emma onto the tailgate. She yelps in surprise.

"If you reach back, you can feel a mattress. Just slide back onto it." I give her instructions. She hesitantly taps her hands along the metal until they hit the soft mattress. She lifts up and slides back. I take off her shoes before they hit the mattress and then follow suit by shedding my trainers and climbing on the makeshift bed next to her.

"Lay back," I whisper. When she hesitates, I add, "Trust me." She takes a deep breath but eventually relaxes onto the mattress and crosses her hands on her tummy. I give her a chaste kiss and whisper, "Close your eyes and only open them when I tell you to." She nods. I remove the blindfold and stroke her hair back.

"Now."

Chapter 12

Emma

My heart is hammering. I have no clue what he has planned. All I know is that I am lying on a mattress in the back of his truck. Definitely not what I had expected on our second date.

When he gives me the signal, I open my eyes and immediately forget to breathe. I don't know where we are, but thousands of stars shine bright above me. The Milky Way stretches over the dark outlines of the hills surrounding us.

"My friend Chris has a field at one of the areas that are a dark sky site. So I borrowed his car and thought we could picnic under the stars." Alex explains, looking at me for a reaction.

I don't know what to say. My feelings are completely overwhelming me. I can feel a tear form in the corner of my eye. I grab his shirt and pull him down to me. My lips mould to his, and I hope my passion proves to him how much this means to me.

"I take it this is a good surprise." He chuckles when I reluctantly release his lips so we can both catch our breath.

"The best," I sigh. Alex rests next to me, and we just look at the stars. Neither of us is saying anything. I feel for his hand on the mattress next to me, and when I find it, I link our fingers. Nobody has ever done something like this for me, and I need to touch him to make sure he is real. We lay there for a while. Neither of us says anything, but we don't need to. It is a comfortable silence. It all is just perfect. And as the word perfect invades my brain, doubts follow straight after.

"Why are you doing this for me?" I ask, my voice only a whisper in the night.

"I wanted to do something that makes you happy." It is a simple explanation but not one that makes sense in my mind.

"I just don't get it." My gaze is directed at the sky. "All my life, people have told me I am not good enough the way I am.

I should be thinner, more serious, more grown up. I am too geeky. I am wasting my time with the flower shop. Whatever I do, say or even think, people, friends, boyfriends, and my mother foremost, tell me everything about me is wrong and I should change. Until you come along: a funny, caring, incredibly handsome guy who can have anyone. Yet you make all this fuss about me. It just doesn't add up." I say, frustrated. I can feel a painful knot in my tummy. I am just waiting for him to agree and see the error he has made.

During my speech, he tensed up next to me. I hear him take a deep breath. Eventually, he turns to me and props his head up on one hand. His other hand lands on my tummy.

"You have no idea how angry this makes me feel." He lifts his hand to my chin and turns my head so he can look into my eyes. "You are an amazing woman. Funny, interesting, beautiful. Anyone who has ever made you feel any different is not worthy of being in your life." His eyes are stubbornly locked on me as if he is trying to see into my soul.

"The truth is that I kind of like the way I am. At home. Behind my walls. I think I can look cute sometimes. I like my geeky side and my passion. But when I step out of my house, I see myself through other people's eyes, and there is nothing cute or interesting," I confess to him. I have never told this to anyone. I know with the body positive movement, I am supposed to accept myself as I am. But it is not that easy. Especially not if you are surrounded by people who are determined to make you believe you should change.

"You are the most fascinating woman I have ever met. And you have been on my mind all week. I am crazy about you, and all I want to do is spend time with you. I want to learn everything about you. And I want this time to be memorable for you, for us. This is why I have put this date together. You deserve to be treated special because you are special." His voice is soft but full of conviction. The knots in my tummy have turned into butterflies. My heart is racing, and warmth spreads through me. I want to believe him. Truth be told, at this moment in time, I do believe him. I am sure my inner demons will rear their ugly heads at some point, but he has managed to silence them for now.

I reach out and push a lock from his forehead. My fingers find their way into his hair, and I pull him down to me. For an eternity, he just hovers millimetres from my lips, his warm breath caressing my skin. I bridge the last gap, and we kiss. It is not an urgent or heated kiss. It is a kiss that is deep and meaningful. I am lost in the moment. I can feel just him. I can taste only him. And he is all I smell. He presses his body to mine, and I can feel his hard cock. It is clear that he at least wants me physically.

He growls when I nibble on his bottom lip. When we break apart, the mood has changed. It just feels like I am exactly where I am supposed to be.

A chilly wind blows across the meadow, and a shiver races through me. Alex asks me to lift my butt and pulls the duvet we had been lying on over us. I slowly start to feel warmer, but I need more heat. And I know where to find it. I scooch closer to him. He pulls me in his arms, and I cuddle against his chest.

"I wish I could stop time," I whisper. "This is as perfect as it gets," I admit with a sigh.

"We can stay here all night," he replies. I know he means the words exactly as he says them. I trust him fully and know he has no ulterior motives. But I want more. I can feel a need grow in me so strong it is almost overwhelming. I can't remember ever feeling like this when being with a man. I lift my head from his chest and look down at him. He softly pushes a stray hair away from my face. My lips connect with his, and I straddle his lap. What starts as a soft kiss quickly turns passionate and oh-so-hot. He flips me so that I am on my back, and he hovers above me. I reach around his waist and pull his body down to me so that we touch, and I can feel him up close and personal again. His hard cock rubs up against my core, and I grind my hips to increase the pressure. He growls, and his lips trail a path to that sensitive spot just below my ear.

"I didn't bring you here for this," he exclaims and tries to push himself up.

"Alex, I need you," I say firmly and place a soft kiss on his Adam's apple, "But if you don't want, that's..." The rest of the sentence is cut off by Alex's lips on mine. His tongue invades me, and he plunders my mouth.

"How can you possibly think I don't want to when my hard cock is pressed against your pussy," he growls and to emphasise his words, he pushes harder against me. He kisses me deeply and urgently and then explores along my jaw down the column of my throat to just below my ear again. I try to stifle a moan when his tongue licks me there.

"Don't hold back. It's just us," he whispers in my ear and licks me again. This time a long moan fills the silence of the night. My hands are on his back and are desperately pulling on his shirt. He briefly sits back on his haunches and pulls his T-shirt over his head. As if called by the siren song, I reach out with my hands. My fingers trace his chest muscles and slide over his abs. He is perfection, and Michelangelo could have used him as a model for his David statue.

My explorations are stopped when he grabs hold of my fingers and pushes my hands above my head. His eyes are dark and hooded with lust.

"Don't move," Alex commands. He then leans down, slides my shirt up and places a kiss on my soft tummy. He licks his way up between my breasts before sucking a hard nipple through my bra. Pleasure radiates through me, and I find it difficult to breathe. He pulls my shirt off me, and, in a swift move, my bra also disappears. A gentle breeze strokes over my breasts before his hot lips suck a nipple into his mouth. One hand, in the meanwhile, explores the other nipple.

He alternates between stroking my breasts, licking my neck and kissing my lips. I am ready to explode, and I am still wearing my trousers. He softly bites one of my nipples, and I moan loudly. My hands stroke through his hair, and he growls.

"You drive me crazy," he mumbles. He kisses a trail down my tummy until he gets to my trousers. All my nerves and insecurities have disappeared, at least for now. I just want more. I need more.

He stops and looks at me. He waits for my go-ahead. I just nod. Frankly, if he would stop now, I might have to kill him. He unbuttons my jeans and pulls the zipper down. Painfully slow, he peels my trousers off and removes my knickers simultaneously.

He then decides to briefly ignore the flesh he has exposed, and instead, he returns to plunder my mouth with a long kiss. This gives me the opportunity to unbutton his trousers, and I push them over his arse. I feel the heat emanating from him as my fingers slide over his bare skin, and a shiver races through me again. He frees himself from his jeans and comes back to me in just boxer briefs. There is no way to hide that he wants me because a formidable erection is stretching his boxers.

My pussy contracts with need at the thought of him inside me, and I desperately try to pull him closer. With a grin, he slowly shakes his head and instead returns to kissing my tummy. He kisses a trail around my belly button before extending his explorations lower. He places a kiss on my mound and the breath escaping his mouth drifts over my sensitive flesh like the wind caressing the mountain tops. My clit is pulsing with need, and I want his lips there. But just when I think he will give me what I seek, he moves his lips to the inside of my right knee. As if he has all the time in the world, he kisses his way up to my pussy. I can feel him so close to where I need him so desperately. Yet again, before he touches the promised land, he stops, moves down to my left knee, and repeats his painful journey.

I am delirious with need and moan, "Alex, please." But he shows no mercy. He alternates between my two legs, so close to where I really want him but still so far. Eventually, I have enough, and my hands, which have been stroking through his hair, grab on and pull him upwards towards my pussy. I am not sure what has come over me, but for once, I am not thinking, just feeling. And I want to feel him sucking my clit and giving me some release.

He chuckles when I manoeuvre him where I need him, and the vibrations emanating from his lips make me shudder. Lazily he takes a lick of my folds and then another before holding me open with one hand. He teases me with his tongue and his fingers. He slowly circles my clit but never touches it.

"So wet, just for me." I hear him whisper.

"Alex," I scream louder than I meant to, and he finally has pity on me. He sucks the sensitive little nub in his mouth, and at the same time, two fingers enter my pussy and curl upwards. As he touches my two super sensitive spots, an orgasm rips through me like I have never experienced before. I try to draw in some air as wave after wave of pleasure shoot through me. I see stars and not the ones in the sky. I am vaguely aware that I am holding his face to me in an attempt to get as much pleasure out of this as I possibly can.

After what feels like the sweetest forever, I am finally returning to reality. My body slumps into the mattress, and I slowly can focus again. My arms and legs feel like jelly, and my nerve endings are on high alert, making every kiss Alex places on my body feel ten times more intense.

"That was so beautiful," he says whilst looking into my eyes. I pull him down to me again and kiss him urgently. I hook a leg around his waist and pull him to me, rubbing myself against him.

"I need you," I say with newfound confidence.

"Emma, I didn't bring condoms with me. We can do this another time."

"My handbag."

"What?" he asks and frowns at me.

"I brought a condom," I whisper, and a blush spreads on my cheek.

"You thought I would try to get you into bed?"

I shake my head.

"No, I thought if this date is anything like the last, I might want to." I try to bury my face in his shoulder.

He seeks out my eyes and kisses me passionately when he sees the truth in them. I can see what my words mean to him, and I feel a little angry with myself that I ever doubted him. He sits up and reaches through the back window. He grabs my bag and gives it to me to get out a condom. He strips off his boxers, and my eyes zoom in on his cock. My fingers itch to reach out and touch him, but then I hesitate.

"Are you sure?" he asks and pulls me out of my thoughts after he has rolled the protection on. He looks at me to make sure this is what I want.

"Yes, Alex. I want you. I want you now," I whisper.

He kisses me long and hard and then rolls on top of me. He groans loudly as he enters me, but he moves slowly, allowing my body to adjust to his sizable dick. But I don't want to go slow. I grab onto his arse cheeks and urge him on until he buries himself in me to the hilt. Once he fills me completely, he lowers his head to my neck and stills.

"Give me a moment," he begs through heavy breathing. Clearly, this feels as good for him as it does for me. After a few seconds, he laces the fingers of his left hand with mine and brings it above my head. He uses this as an anchor whilst pumping into me. At first, he moves at a slow pace, but once I lock my legs behind his back, his self-control breaks, and he takes what he needs. He creates amazing friction between us, and I can feel a welcoming pressure start to grow within me again. I put my feet on the mattress and lift my hips in sync to meet him every time he sinks into me. This new angle allows his cock to hit me just at the right spot. I feel another orgasm approaching when Alex reaches between us and strokes my clit. Like lightning, the release rushes through me, and I call out his name again. His grunts become louder and louder until he pushes hard into me and cries out. I feel his hardness pulse in me, and his body jerks until he collapses on top of me

Chapter 13

Alex

I am breathing heavily with my head in the crook of her neck. I slowly push myself up to look at her before bending down again and kissing her softly. I can't get enough of her taste or her smell. I roll off her and get rid of the condom before pulling the duvet back over us. She cuddles against my chest.

"Emms, you still haven't opened your eyes," I chuckle.

"I'm scared that if I open my eyes, I will find out it was all just a dream."

"No dream," I reassure her. She finally looks at me and softly strokes through my hair. I kiss her on top of her head and pull her even closer. I realise we never ate the picnic I brought, but I don't think either of us wants to move from our embrace. Above us glimmer the stars. The only noises are the insects singing and the vegetation swaying in the wind. In my arms is the most amazing woman I have ever met. Life is perfect at this moment.

***

A ringing fills the air, and my eyes open on instinct. I realise that I must have fallen asleep. I softly shift Emma onto the mattress, sit up and reach for my trousers which I had pushed to the side. I rummage in my jeans pocket and pull my phone out.

"Hello?" I whisper.

"Alex, this is Jonathan from FMR. We are calling in your team for a search and rescue. Two tourists are missing up on Horse Pike." Jonathan is not from my team. He and three other volunteers cover the emergency phone for call-outs and will coordinate a rescue mission where required.

"Now?" I ask, knowing quite well that Jonathan wouldn't have called if it wasn't urgent. During the day, we usually just get a text sent to our phone by an automated message service. However, if there is a rescue at night, we get a call to ensure we don't miss it. And the guys covering the emergency line know to only call if it is a genuine emergency.

"They didn't come down last night, but their drunk buddies have been partying until now and only realised thirty minutes ago that the two are missing." He explains impatiently. He probably needs to call the rest of the team, so the last thing he wants is to have a discussion with me.

"Where are we meeting?"

"Hill Road, next to the Kendall Farm. They were supposed to come down that way. A helicopter is already out searching with thermal imaging."

"I'll be there in forty minutes," I confirm before saying goodbye. The clock on my phone shows me that it is just after four in the morning. I look longingly at Emma. What would I give to curl around her, pull the duvet up and hold her until sunrise, but sadly, I don't have that option. I have to pop home and get my gear and drop Emma off at her cottage. Luckily, there is no traffic at this time of the day, so we should make it back to Fellside in twenty minutes, giving me just enough time to make it to the meeting point. Before I pull my T-Shirt over my head, I look at Emma again. She is hugging the duvet with her delicious bottom sticking out. I love being a mountain rescue volunteer, but at this moment in time, I would give everything if I weren't.

I slowly stroke her hair and kiss her jaw. "Emms," I whisper in her ear. She stirs but doesn't open her eyes.

"Emma," I say a little louder, and her eyelids slowly lift. She grins, and my dick takes this as an invitation for round two.

I groan, "Don't look at me like this. It makes me want to take you again, but sadly I have to leave." Her beautiful smile turns into a frown. *Yup, I hate my volunteer role at the moment.*

"Mountain Rescue called. Two tourists are missing." I place a soft kiss on her neck. Sleepily she reaches out and strokes my cheek.

"Okay, let me get dressed," she agrees immediately and reaches for any clothes she can reach without leaving the warmth of the duvet. We quickly get dressed, and Emma helps me cover up the mattress. I hold the passenger door open for her. However, she doesn't get in. Instead, she looks up at the sky again and sighs. Her warm lips find mine.

"Best date ever," she says with a grin before hopping into the car.

**

I make it to the meeting point just in time. Everyone else is already there and gathered around the two specialist off-roader cars FMR uses to get higher up the hills than your average truck can make it.

"How come you are the last one here? You only live down the lane," Phil asks as I step up next to him. The others don't pay us much attention and, instead, are putting away their backpacks in the cars.

"I wasn't home last night," I reply as quietly as possible without whispering. I am not ashamed of what happened last night. On the contrary, I would love to shout it out to the world to hear that this amazing woman finds me worthy of letting me hold her in my arms. But this is all new, and I would like to keep it between Emma and me until she feels assured that I am serious about her. I will tell Phil everything later, but I don't need the rest of the team gossiping.

"Wasn't it supposed to be just a date?" he replies, equally quiet. He adds air quotes to the last three words.

"I'll tell you later. For now, let's just focus on these two tourists." I shut him up. Phil grins at me. He knows me too well. If I don't brag about a woman, then this is not my usual tag'em and drop'em game. I put my backpack on and walk over to Tommy, who is waiting for us, so he can give us a situation update.

"Alright, mate?" Nick greets me before smirking at me in a rather weird way as I join the group assembled around Tommy. This can't be good. I am sure he is up to something. But before I can ask him, Tommy calls our attention, and we all go into rescue mode, turning our focus to the situation at hand.

It takes us an hour to locate the tourists and another hour to get to them. They are hungry and show mild hypothermia symptoms but are otherwise okay. They were at least smart enough to look for shelter and huddled under a rock overhang. There is no need for a helicopter, so we walk them down the mountain, where an ambulance awaits them to take them to the hospital for a quick check-up.

We all gather at the rescue centre for a short briefing. Where possible, we try to debrief straight after each mission as our memory is still fresh. But Tommy has mercy with us today. Looking at all the sleep-deprived faces, he keeps the meeting short and finally releases us. My stomach rumbles loudly, and rather than going to my car, I hit the fridge in the small galley-style kitchen. There are always cakes or similar snacks in it, which supporters of FMR regularly drop off.

The last time I had food was yesterday at lunchtime. The picnic I had prepared for Emma and me is currently sitting at home in the cooler. I grin to myself when I remember what enjoyable activity stopped us from eating it.

It is now close to nine in the morning. If I am quick with my shower, I can make it to work almost on time, and that should mean I have time to pop to Emma's and surprise her with lunch.

"Alex, mate, I was walking past a certain florist earlier this week, and who should I see snogging in there: you!" Nick pulls me out of my thoughts. He is leaning against the kitchen door. Jonathan, who raised the alarm earlier and is currently making coffee, is pretending to not hear us.

"So what?" I ask. Nick is trying to get a rise out of me, and I refuse to give him what he wants. He has always been difficult, and he will always be difficult. And I don't know why. As a kid, he would run after my friends and me and try to hang out but then rat us out to teachers or our parents if we had played a prank on someone. And he seemed to have a particular issue with me. I was concerned when we were assigned to the same team at FMR, but to be honest, you can rely on this guy one hundred percent when it comes to mountain rescue. The rest of the time, I just try to ignore him.

"Well, I didn't have you down as a chubby chaser. What, no luck with the pretty girls anymore?" Nick chuckles about his own joke and mimes to Jonathan the outline of massive hips and breasts. Jonathan, clearly uncomfortable about this conversation, returns his attention to making coffee.

I close the fridge door with a slam and start walking towards Nick, but Phil is suddenly beside me with his hand on my shoulder. I'm not sure where he has come from, but I am glad he is here now because I was only a fraction of seconds away from planting my fist in Nick's face. I don't care what he thinks of me, but nobody disrespects this remarkable woman who has been hurt so much.

"Don't let him get to you." Phil tries to calm me down. Nick smirks. He knows he has me where he wants me. He should just take the win and walk away. But, as always, he doesn't know when to stop.

"You know what, she did look like she knows how to use her mouth. Maybe I should get some flowers today and see if I can find out if she is willing to use her lips on other body parts than just the face." He chuckles with a glint in his eyes.

I jump forward, too quick for Phil to react, and grab Nick by his shirt. I push him against the wall.

"Stay the fuck away from her!" I scream in his face. I can feel someone pulling me backwards away from the little weasel. It must be Phil, as Jonathan is positioning himself between Nick and me to create a barrier. I try to pull free from Phil. All I can think of is to wipe the smirk off Nick's face. But Phil is stronger than I thought he would be and manages to get me to the other side of the tight space.

"What the fuck is going on here?" Tommy steps into the kitchen. I ignore him. Surprisingly, Nick doesn't rat me out either. We just stare at each other.

"I love her, you fucking idiot. If you just as much as glance in her direction, I swear to God—" I shout, leaving the threat hanging in the air. It is dead quiet in the kitchen, and four pairs of eyes stare at me.

"What?" I ask.

Nick shakes his head and walks out of the kitchen. Tommy slaps me on the back and warns me to stop fighting before he and Jonathan follow Nick.

"You love her?" Phil asks me. This is when I realise what I have just said. Do I love her? I don't have to ponder this question long. Yes, yes, I do. I am crazy about her. Last night was incredible, but there is so much more. I want to spend every spare minute with her. My mind keeps wandering to things I want to do or see with her in a year, two years, or ten years' time. I am seeing her in my future. No, scratch this. I can't actually imagine a future without her. This should scare me. I have never done the love thing; I was never sure if love even existed. And I have only known her for such a short period of time. But somehow, this all doesn't matter.

"Yes, I do," I sigh, and a small smile spreads across my face, "But I haven't told her yet." Phil and I lock eyes, and he can see that these are not just words. This is the truth.

Phil grins. "Let me go and take a shower and then we can go for breakfast, and you can tell me what the fuck happened last night that turned this eternal bachelor into the happily ever after guy."

Chapter 14

Emma

It is difficult to wipe the smile off my face. I still can't believe what happened yesterday, what I allowed to happen... But it felt right. So right.

"I love you, and I'm super happy for you, but you have to turn the satisfied grin down," Christina says when we devour our lunch. As usual, we just have a sandwich in the backroom. "You are making me jealous. I want some action too," She whines. "I think I have to turn up my flirting with Bambi a notch."

"Please! He already doesn't know where to run to when he sees you coming." I giggle.

"I will wear him down. Mark my words!" she declares as the bell above the door chimes.

"Why don't I pop to the bakery for some éclairs? Giving you a break from my grin," I suggest. Christina gives me a thumbs up.

"But get me the big gooey caramel one," she demands.

I grab some cash from our tip box on the till and wave goodbye to Christina, who is helping two women with potted plants. The bakery is at the top of the town, and I enjoy the short walk in the crisp air. The sun is out, which isn't a given here in the Lake District. We have more rain than not, but at least that keeps the fields and woods green and lush.

The Cherry Pie Bakery is known for its éclairs and is popular with tourists and locals alike. I join the short queue that has snaked its way onto the pavement. The bakery itself is not very big and more than three people waiting means the line spills out onto the street. I'm standing behind a couple in hiking gear. I'm guessing they are tourists as I have never seen them before. I am about to text Alex when I hear a sentence that makes me listen up.

"Yes, I heard the rumours about Alex," the woman ahead of the tourist couple says to her friend standing next to her.

"I mean, seriously, why is he dating her? She is so not his type. Do you remember his last girlfriend? What was her name? Sandy? Sally? The one from Kendal. Now she was a looker." Her friend giggles. Of course, it could be a different Alex, but in my guts, I know they are talking about my Alex. I can feel the heat creeping into my cheeks, and I duck behind the couple in front of me.

"Veronica said she saw them both at that new Arabic place in town, and she ordered shit loads of food," the woman continues.

Her friend bursts out laughing and adds, "Like she really needs it." They both giggle. Self-consciously, I pull on my top to hide more of my backside.

"Honestly, either he has a bet going, or he has fallen on his head on one of his climbs. But she is just so not right for him." The two women shake their heads in unison. I feel sick to my stomach. My heart is trying to hold on to the memories of last night, but my brain is starting to take over. I had successfully ignored the doubts my brain spewed, but after what I have just heard, my heart is no longer winning this battle. *They are right. What am I doing? He can do so much better than me.*

I turn and quickly leave the queue. I slowly walk back to the shop. As I enter, Christina takes one look at me and runs towards me.

"What happened? Are you alright? You look like you saw death," she asks in a panic.

I try to smile. "All okay. They ran out of éclairs."

"Come on, that can't be it."

"Would you mind if I take the rest of the day off?" I ask, "I am super tired from yesterday."

Christina looks at me suspiciously.

"No problem, but are you sure you are okay?" she asks again. I just nod, grab my bag and leave without another word.

I do feel tired suddenly. Very tired. I just want to curl up in bed and sleep through this pain. I feel my phone vibrating and pull it out of my bag just as I open the door to my house. The display shows Alex's name. I take a deep breath and answer.

"Hi," is all I say.

"Is it crazy that I miss you already?" he chuckles instead of a standard greeting.

"It's just the post-coital euphoria. Doesn't mean anything," I say flatly.

"Post-coital what?" he asks.

"Never mind. Listen, Alex, yesterday was great, but we both know this will run its course sooner rather than later, so maybe we should just leave it and avoid further complications in the future," I say quietly. There is silence on the other end.

"Alex?"

"I'm here," he says, and I can hear some anger in his voice. "But I'm not sure what to say to this bullshit. We had an amazing night, what we had—no, what we have is the real deal, and you just give me this crap and break up over the phone with me? What happened?"

Tears start to run down my cheek, and I lean against the door behind me. I take a deep breath to try and get my voice under control.

"Nothing. I just took a good look in the mirror and realised this was not real. Trust me, you will wake up in a few weeks and wonder what you are doing with me. You are an amazing man, and you can get anyone you want. You deserve better."

"I can't believe we are there again!" His voice is strangled, like he is trying not to shout at me. "I thought you finally trusted me."

I say nothing. I do trust him and he might really feel like he is falling for me now. But that will change, and there is no way I would survive the heartache when he finally sees sense if I let this carry on. Even now, it's already tearing me apart. A few more weeks with him, and it will kill me. Rip off the plaster and end it now. Makes the most sense. My brain has spoken.

"Alex, I have to go," I whisper. I hear, "Emma—" just before I press the button to end the call. I hover over his name. I should block his number, but I can't get myself to do it. And let's face it, what's the point? We live in a tiny village, and there is no escaping him.

Instead, I switch my phone off and drag myself to my bedroom. On the way there, I shed all my clothes. I crawl into my bed naked and pull my duvet over my head. I want to block out the noise, the light, reality, and the world. I just want to sleep.

Chapter 15

Alex

I stare at my phone. *What. The. Actual. Fuck.* She did not just put the phone down on me. I try to call her back, but the call goes to voicemail. What happened? I sit in the small meeting room at the rescue centre and stare at my phone. After the trouble with Nick, I needed to hear her voice. The rescue centre has only one bathroom, so whilst waiting for Phil to finish his shower, I made the call. But this is not where I had seen this go.

"Listen, Alex," I hear Nick behind me. "I am sorry about what I said." He continues as he steps up to the table. I just stare at him.

"What happened?" he asks, concerned when he sees the look on my face.

"Fuck knows. She just broke up with me." I'm not sure why I am telling him, but I need to say it out loud to believe it.

"What, why?"

"If I knew that, I would not be talking to you but would be out there fixing it." I shake my head. I feel numb. Memories of last night flood back in my mind, and with them comes my fighting spirit.

"Nick, tell Phil I had to go." I push past him. I really have no time for him now. I take two stairs at once and run to my car once I make it to the ground floor. I have barely closed my door when I turn the key in the ignition and pull out of the car park. I have to remind myself to stick to the snail-like speed limit in Fellside because all my foot wants to do is press the gas pedal to the floor. When I finally get to the flower shop, I, of course, can't find a car park. I illegally park in front of the library on double yellow lines. Who gives a fuck if I get a ticket? I pull the door open to Emma's shop and shout at Christina, "Where is she?"

"What did you do?" she sasses back.

"Me, nothing."

"Well, she went to the bakery happy as a Teletubby on E and returned completely deflated."

"What time was that?" I pace the shop floor.

"Forty minutes, half an hour ago," Christina just stands there and looks at me. I can see that she is still not sure if I haven't messed this up.

"I only spoke with her twenty minutes ago. Before that, I saw her this morning. That was it."

"Oh good, she spoke to you. Maybe she really was just tired." She seemingly relaxes.

"No, she fucking wasn't," I shout, and Christina flinches at the tone of my voice. "She broke up with me."

"What?" Christina whispered. Her eyes go wide, and she looks genuinely shocked. "I don't understand," she adds.

"Well, that makes two of us," I reply, throwing my hands in the air. "I need to see her. Where is she?"

"What did she say to you?"

"I will soon realise I can do better than her, and she'd rather break up now. Or something along those lines. Where is she, Christina?" I beg.

"Someone must have said something to her that brought her insecurities back," Christina says, ignoring my question again.

"Christina, where the fuck is she?" I hiss.

"Probably in her cottage," she finally answers me. But before I can storm out of the shop, she stops me. "Alex, don't give up on her. I know she hurt you today and probably will hurt you again when she finally faces you, but the way her mother and her friends," the last word she marks with air quotes, "have treated her, has broken Emma. Something or someone must have triggered these ugly thoughts to come back." She looks at me with fear in her eyes. I am glad Emma has at least one true friend. I nod to show her that I understand. I had already promised myself to not give up.

I storm out of the shop and run around the corner to Emma's cottage. When I finally reach her door, I take a deep breath before knocking. There is no reply to my first knock, so I hit the wooden door harder. No reply. Now I am getting desperate. I continually knock and shout, "Emma, open up." I do not give up that easily.

After what feels like an eternity, I hear the lock engage, and the door opens. Emma looks pale except for the red rings around her puffy eyes. She is wearing a bathrobe and I guess not much else. But now is not the time to appreciate her lack of clothing.

"Alex, what are you doing here?"

I grab the wall on either side of the door to stop myself from pushing into her house.

"What am I doing here? What do you think I am doing here? You put the phone down on me, and I don't accept you breaking up with me."

"Alex," she whispers. "I can't." A tear trickles down her face. She is hurting, I can see it. I reach out to wipe the tear away, but she takes a step back.

"Please go," her voice barely audible. All my instincts tell me to fight, to force her to speak to me, *heck*, this is what I came for. But I also know I am not calm enough to talk to her when she is vulnerable. I need to give her and me time to think.

"Emma," I say to get her to look at me, "I will go for now. But let me tell you something: this is not the end. We will talk, and I will show you that you are wrong. This," and I point between her and me, "this is right. And I won't let your past destroy our future." At least she knows now how I feel.

She looks at me. She slowly lifts her hand as if she wants to touch me but then realises what she is doing and pulls her hand back.

"Bye, Alex," she says and closes the door.

"This is not over," I shout at the closed door, knowing she can hear me.

Chapter 16

Emma

It has been a week, a miserable week, since my dream came crashing down. The shop is quiet. Christina is typing away on some social media posts. She tried to get me to talk to her about the breakup, but I just shrugged it off and withdrew behind my walls. Alex has been to the shop a few times, and he has texted and called. But when he comes over, I usually flee through the back entrance, and I ignore his calls and texts. I have yet to face him again.

Christina keeps telling me that he is miserable. But I am sure he will find someone to take his mind off it soon. And me, I just feel dead inside. Occasionally my heart comes through and tries to convince me that I got this all wrong, but then my brain kicks in and my walls are back up.

"Do you want me to get us some lunch?" I ask Christina. She looks up from her computer.

"No, you know what, I so have had enough of this atmosphere. I need to get out of here for a while. I'll have lunch in the pub. I'll bring you a sandwich back." With this declaration, she grabs her bag and leaves the shop.

Unsure, I look at the door. I am tempted to close the store while she is away to avoid dealing with customers—or with Alex if he decides exactly now to make another attempt to talk to me. But I can't just lock up in the middle of the day. As I am hovering between the door and the back room, trying to decide what to do, the door opens and a guy who looks familiar steps in.

I try to put my best customer service fake smile on, "Hi, can I help you?"

"Nope, I think I might be able to help you," he replies.

"Are you a sales rep from some company? We are not looking for new suppliers." I cut him off.

He chuckles. "No, my name is Nick. I volunteer with Alex at FMR." When he sees me tense up, he adds, "He doesn't know I am here."

I take a deep breath. But then his words sink in, and I am even more confused. If Alex hasn't sent him, what does he want from me?

"Has Alex told you about me?" he asks. I nod. Alex told me about most of his teammates when we were at dinner.

"Well, then, you know Alex and I are no friends." Sadness creeps into his eyes when he says this. He puts his hands in his jacket pocket. "Alex is miserable. I have never seen him like this. I don't know what happened between the two of you, but whatever he did wrong, you should give him another chance," he declares. I am stunned. Why would he come here and tell me this? I wonder if he lied and Alex did send him. But then, he is right. Alex had told me that aside from rescue missions, those two don't see eye to eye.

"He can do better than me," I blurt out. Nick looks at me bewildered.

"Who told you that bullshit?" he asks. I don't know what to tell him. I feel I have already said way too much.

"Hey, I admit, Alex did date these model barbie type women in the past, and you are," I stiffen and get ready for his harsh words, "a natural beauty," he finishes the sentence. "If you ask me if anyone can do better, it is you. But you are what he needs. I have known Alex all my life, and I have never seen him like this. He declared in front of us that he loves you. Alex doesn't do love."

I take a deep breath.

"Why are you telling me this? Why do you care?" My voice is harsher than I meant it to be. He runs his fingers through his dark hair.

"When we were kids, I wanted to be Alex's friend. But whatever I tried, I didn't seem to fit into his group of mates, and they ignored me." He shrugs. "So I started to get his attention by pissing him off. I tried to change my behaviour the last few years, but he usually just brushes any attempt from me to be friendly aside, and then the old me comes through again." The look on his face tells me he has just shared something with me, he has never told anyone before. I am not sure why he feels he can trust me with his story. There is the chance that he trying to use me to get in with Alex but seeing the sincerity on his face, I don't think he is.

"I'm sorry." I am not specific about what I am sorry about, but I think he knows that I understand what it is to live with inner demons that stop you from getting what you want.

"Yeah, well, I'm working on it." He laughs nervously.

"If you want proof of how serious this is, Alex has resigned from FMR," he explains, bringing the spotlight back to Alex and me. I gasp. I know how much Alex loves his mountain rescue work.

"Why?" It just doesn't make sense.

"He says he can't focus, which could put people at risk. Tommy has not accepted his resignation and has just taken him off the roster. But for him to give up the rescue work made me realise how much he is hurting. I had to do something. I thought if I, the most unlikely defender, would come and talk to you, you might give him a chance." He gives me a nervous grin.

I look at him in silence. I'm not sure what to say to this. My heart is hammering. Why exactly did I think the hurtful words of some random women I have never met were more real than the words of a man who has only been truthful to me?

"Well, I'll go then," Nick says and points towards the exit when I remain silent.

"Nick, wait," I call just before he opens the door. I step toward him and then hug him. I am not a hugger, but this moment called for one. He stiffens for a moment and then returns the hug.

"Thank you for coming here. I think you may have gained his attention the right way this time. You have proven to be a friend to him," I say.

He smiles, nods at me and turns towards the door.

"Oh crap," he exclaims, and I follow his line of sight. Alex is standing at the other side of the road staring at us. Well, not so much starring but shooting daggers at us. We all stand still for a few seconds before Alex storms off.

"You were saying." Nick laughs again nervously, "Emma, do you do funeral flowers? Because I think he will kill me…"

I giggle. "I will go and talk to him."

The minute I say the words, my heart starts to beat like I have just finished a marathon. So not only do I have to talk to him about my dramatic breakup, but I also have to explain why Nick hugged me. And my inner demons are still battling my heart. *I really want to go back to bed.*

Chapter 17

Alex

I enter my workshop shaking with anger.

"Boss, that was quick," my apprentice says as he sees me. I don't pay him any attention. I grab a piece of wood lying on a workbench, and it takes everything in me to not throw it across the room.

"Gary, go for lunch," I hiss at my apprentice. I see he wants to argue, as he usually eats his lunch here, but the look on my face makes him change his mind. He grabs his thermos lunch bag and walks out the door.

I was on the way to a client when I saw Christina walking into the pub. Emma had to be alone in the shop; now she would have to talk to me. And so I turned my car around and walked to the shop once I found a car park close by. Before I could cross the road, I caught sight of her hugging Nick. *What was that wanker doing there? Since when did he even know her? Was he the real reason she broke up with me?* When they both saw me and looked shocked, I had my answer.

My insides are in turmoil. I want to be angry, but at the same time, I can't believe it, and my stupid heart tries to convince me that I should find out first what really happened. In an attempt to distract myself, I grab the phone and call the client whose appointment I have missed to give him some kind of excuse.

It takes me ten minutes of grovelling to convince the client to give me another chance. I will have to do some free overtime over the weekend, but that should make him happy. I put the phone down when I hear a shuffling sound behind me.

"I thought I told you to go for lunch," I snarl and turn around. Only it isn't Gary: it's Emma. She stands at the entrance to my workshop. Her hands nervously grip the hem of her shirt. She looks at me with large sad eyes.

"Hi," she says with a wobble in her voice.

"What do you want?" I ask. There is anger in my voice but also pain.

"Alex, I think we need to talk."

I laugh cynically. "Now you want to talk."

"Nick came to ask me to give you another chance," she explains. I freeze. There are about ten thousand things wrong with this sentence.

"What? Bullshit."

"I am serious. He said he had never seen you like this. He told me that you quit FMR."

"Why would he care?"

"That's a question you should ask him. But the hug you saw was me saying thank you to him. Nothing more."

I nod. I want to be stubborn like she has been. I want to be cold and hurt her as much as she has hurt me. And just as this thought enters my brain, I immediately realise it is not true: I don't want to hurt her, I want to hold her. I want her in my life.

"What did you tell him?" I ask, my voice noticeably calmer.

"That you didn't do anything wrong. I heard some women talk about how you can do so much better, and my old insecurities came back," she finally offers me some explanation. Some women. I don't care who they were. I hope karma gets them.

"Who was talking?" I hiss and step closer to her. I am close enough for her to put her hands on my chest.

"It doesn't matter. I don't know them," she says softly.

"And you believed them over me?" I should be angry, but I just feel sad.

"Yes," she nods with a sombre look on her face. "In the past, the few times people did tell me nice things, it was usually a take-down dressed up as a compliment." A lone tear runs down her face. "I don't know how to handle genuine compliments. I am programmed to distrust them and trust only when people are mean. I am sorry, I am so messed up," she sobs. By now, the tears are free-flowing, and her hands are shaking. I can't take it any longer. I step forward and pull her in my arms. She slides her hands around my waist and buries her face in my shoulder. I softly stroke her back but let her cry. When she stops shaking, I slowly pull back a little.

"Wait here," I tell her and put a soft kiss on her forehead. I text Gary to take the rest of the day off. Then I lock the door. I grab her hand and pull her to a corner of the workshop where a large item is hidden underneath a piece of cloth.

"I made a present for you, but I didn't have a chance to give it to you yet."

"What is it?" she asks.

I make her stand right in front of it.

"Do you remember when we met, you said you had a mirror, and this is why you know you can't go out with me?" She looks at me and nods. I pull the cloth off.

"I think your mirror is broken. So I made you a new one." She stares at it but says nothing. The frame of the mirror is from the same stained oak as her shelves. It is a simple mirror, nothing fancy, but the mirror image is what I want to show her.

I step behind her so we both appear in the mirror and put my hands around her waist and onto her tummy.

"When I look at you, I see these amazing eyes. Can you see how they are blue like the icy water at the bottom of a glazier?" I reach up and softly swipe the hair away from one side of her neck. "I see this amazing hair that shines golden in the sun. And I see this kissable neck, and all I want to do is lick it and taste it." I let my lips trace from her ear all the way down to where her neck meets her shoulder. Before I continue, I take a deep breath and inhale her scent. I lock eyes with her in the mirror. Tears are rolling down her cheeks again.

My hands cup her breast. "I mean, these are just magnificent." A snort erupts from her before her serious face returns.

"I love every curve and how it feels when I run my fingers over them," I continue whilst my hands slide over her hips. "And I love everything you can't see in the mirror. Your passion for life. Your sense of humour, your quirky nervousness and your incredible intelligence. I love how you make me feel when I am with you." I grab her hips and turn her around, so she faces me.

"There is only one thing I hate." Fear fills her eyes, but I continue, "I hate not having you in my life. I love you, Emma."

She cups my face and slowly pulls me down. She kisses my lips softly and whispers, "I love you too, Alex."

Epilogue

Alex

The last year and a half have been the best of my life. It took me only a few months to convince Emma to move in with me. There really wasn't a point in having two separate places to live when she spent most of her time at my house. And the rent income from her cottage helped us take a trip to Beirut last spring, and now we are on the way to Iceland.

My Emma wants to see the Northern Lights. And I am all in for that. Since we found our way back together, she has blossomed into this confident and amazing woman that blows me away every day. Occasionally her insecurities rear their ugly head. And then I take her to our mirror. I don't even have to say anything anymore. One look, and she finds her way back.

"Where do we catch the bus to the hotel?" she asks nervously. She hates that I planned the whole trip this time. I thought I was doing her a favour by taking this burden off her, but, it turns out, she loves planning trips. She feels she has lost control with me in charge of our travel plans. It makes me chuckle, and I have been teasing my little control freak for the last few weeks. But now is not the time.

"We are not getting a bus. I got us a rental car," I explain. Her eyes light up.

"You are amazing," she declares and stalks towards the booths of the rental car companies. I deal with the paperwork, and an hour later, we are driving out of Reykjavik in our SUV.

"Shouldn't we be heading towards the town centre?" Emma looks from the Satnav to me with a frown.

"Nope."

"Nope. Is that all I get?"

"Yup."

"Argh, you can be so frustrating." She crosses her arms in front of her chest, but when she doesn't object to me putting my hand on her leg, I know she isn't really cross. For the rest of the journey, her eyes are glued to the window, and she is taking in the snowy landscape.

It is November and the days are short so far north. It is almost dark when we stop in front of a small cabin, even if it is only after half past three in the afternoon.

"You booked us a cabin?" Emma announces with excitement in her voice.

"Yup." I grin

"With a hot tub?" she asks.

"Yup," is all I say again. Emma squeals, grabs me and kisses me hard.

"And the forecast for tonight is good. We should see the Northern Lights," I explain, which gets me another kiss. Ever since she discovered that a lot of people in Iceland have a holiday home outside the city with a hot tub, she has dreamed of watching the Northern Lights whilst soaking in the warm water. And that's precisely what I will give her.

We unload the car and unpack our suitcases. The owner of the cabin kindly stocked it for us with food I had ordered, so we spend the rest of the early evening cooking a delicious meal together.

After dinner, we change into bathing suits and head to the hot tub. It is dark by now, and we can see the glittering stars in the sky. It reminds me of our first night together. I can honestly say that my feelings for her were crazy strong then, but have only grown stronger since.

It is freezing cold when we take the bathrobes off. But once we step into the warm water, the cold is forgotten. Emma slides close to me and leans her head on my shoulder.

"Thank you so much. This is amazing."

"You haven't even seen the Northern Lights yet." I chuckle.

"Even if I don't. This is still an amazing trip just because you are here," she whispers.

I smile down at her and kiss her deeply before we return to watch the sky.

"Oh my god, there it is!" she screams excitedly and points into the distance. A faint green ribbon waves across the black canvas of the night. It slowly gets stronger and moves like it is dancing. We are quiet and watch it arm in arm. There are no words to describe this natural wonder. Just like there are no words to describe how deep my love for Emma goes. But that doesn't mean I can't try, right?

"Emma," I whisper in her ear. She pushes closer to me, but her gaze remains directed at the sky.

"Marry me." I have wanted to say these words out loud for weeks.

Emma freezes and then turns. She cups my face.

"Say it again," she demands.

"Marry me. Please." My heart is racing, but her eyes are full of love, and I am confident in her answer.

She nods, and the one word I need to hear tumbles from her lips: "Yes."

I pull her closer and kiss her deeply. I reach for the small ring box I have hidden under a towel on the edge of the hot tub. A simple platinum ring. No stone. She gasps when I put it on her finger. It is precisely what she wanted. My Emma doesn't like diamonds; she always wanted a plain ring that she would reuse as a wedding ring with our initials engraved for the wedding. I heard her tell Christina once and immediately filed it away for future reference.

"Why are you so perfect?" she asks me.

"I am not perfect, but you bring out the best in me."

THANK YOU

Thank you for taking time to read Blossom with Me. Please spare a minute to leave a review on Amazon. Even a short sentence or two helps.

STAY IN TOUCH

Never miss a new release:
Sign up for my newsletter to be the first to hear about free content, new releases, cover reveals, sales, and more:
www.daniebooks.com/sign-up

Follow me on:

Instagram: https://www.instagram.com/dani_elias_books/

Facebook: https://www.facebook.com/DaniEliasBooks

or visit my Website
www.daniebooks.com

FELLSIDE MOUNTAIN RESCUE SERIES

Do you want to meet more guys from the Fellside Mountain Rescue Team?
Fellside Mountain Rescue's volunteers help those that are lost in the mountains. But who will help them when they fall for their women? Meet the guys who risk their lives for others and risk it all when it comes to love.

Pre-order the rest of the series now!

Sing with Me
Book 2 in the Fellside Mountain Rescue Serie

Phil is an introvert who prefers to remain behind the scenes. When he meets Christina, he is torn between his instinct to run and his desire for her. Lucky for him, she is as determined as he is shy. Christina knows she has found the "One". When she finally gets Phil to open up to her, nothing seems to stay in their way until she asks him for something he can't give her.

My name is Phil. I am known for being quiet and shy. It usually takes a lot of alcohol and the help of my wingman Alex to get me anywhere near a woman until I meet Christina. She is loud, bubbly and relentlessly pursuing me. I could drown in her brown eyes and wish nothing more than to give in to her advances. In reality, I usually run the minute she looks in my direction. But she doesn't give up and slowly brings me out of my shell. Then she pushes me too far, and I need to decide if I am brave or retreat to my comfort zone.

Paint with Me
Book 3 in the Fellside Mountain Rescue Serie

Nick is battling his past demons when he meets the woman he has been waiting for all his life. Now he needs to convince her that they are meant to be. Following a messy divorce, Charlotte is weary of men. She has convinced herself that she is past her sell-by date. Why a significantly younger man is pursuing her is beyond her. Should she listen to her heart or trust her gut feeling that something is wrong?

My name is Nick. I have many faults. I tend to rub people up the wrong way, and I know it. I have hurt people in the past, but I am trying to become a better man. Especially when I meet her. With her feisty attitude, she captures my heart. I need her in my life, but my reputation and our age difference are a deal-breaker for her. So what if she is a little older than me? I am determined to show her I have changed and how good we are together. I need help and have to ask the one person I don't want to ask.

Climb with Me

Book 4 in the Fellside Mountain Rescue Serie

Chris knows he messed up, but he doesn't hesitate to use his bond with Suzie's son to convince the single mum that he is the one. Suzie is running from a dark past. When her past catches up, will Chris be there for her and her son, or will he turn his back on them?

My name is Chris. I am not particularly keen to help at the fundraising events the Fellside Mountain Rescue centre regularly hosts. That is until a particular pretty new helper shows up. Suzie has me immediately under her spell. Unfortunately, I accidentally insult her at the first opportunity. It is an honest mistake, but now I look like a chauvinistic pig who believes women belong in the kitchen. It's a good thing that her cute son is on my side. He helps me to get back in his mummy's good books. The closer Suzie and I get, the more I feel she is hiding something. She is scared, and I am determined to protect Suzie and her son from whoever is after them

Read with Me
Book 5 in the Fellside Mountian Rescue Serie

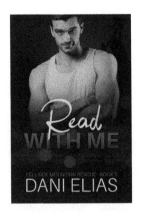

Rob might be a prankster, but he is also observant and thoughtful, a side he tends to only show to special people like Olivia. If only she would see him as more than a prankster. Olivia struggled in school, and to this day, her family won't let her forget that. Can she fight the path her family had put her on and give all the things she wants to experience - including the sexy librarian - a try?

My name is Rob. People usually think I am joking when I tell people that I work at the small library in Fellside. I am not your stereotypical librarian, but I don't believe in stereotypes. My mother thinks I am a man-child, and my mates consider me the joker of the group. I just think life is too short for us not to enjoy every minute. When I meet Olivia, I immediately see her potential and hunger for life, even if she can't see it herself. I make it my goal to open her eyes to all the wonderful possibilities. She fights me all the way, but I am not one to give up.

Build with Me
Book 6 in the Fellside Mountain Rescue Serie

Tommy was never the relationship type of guy. Until he meets Ella. She captivates him with her beauty and intelligence, and he wants the rest of the world to see what a fascinating person she is. Ella is used to doing what is best for the family business. Then she meets Tommy and questions her loyalty towards her family for the first time. When it comes down to it, will she choose her family or take a chance on love?

My name is Tommy. I am a textbook workaholic and have made my hotel the best-rated establishment in Fellside. Plans to expand my hotel bring me face-to-face with Ella. Suddenly, increasing room bookings and maximising revenue from weddings is the last thing on my mind. She is not just beautiful, but she is also a brilliant architect. I hire her family's company for my project, and immediately I realise there is a problem: Someone else is taking credit for her work. I can't let that happen. But how will she react when I put the limelight on her?

Lightning Source UK Ltd.
Milton Keynes UK
UKHW011600020323
417910UK00003B/42